V1 - VIXEN

BY

STEPHEN LIDDELL

First Published 2016.

Copyright © 2016 Stephen Liddell

Front Cover Art and Design by Ru Barard

Front Cover Photo by Gooch Barard Photography

ISBN #: 978-1-326-56491-9

*This book is dedicated to my dear
friend Ru, who is like a sister to me.*

*Thanks for everything and remember
that there would be no V without R(u).*

TABLE OF CONTENTS

Acknowledgements

My thanks go out to all those who helped me create V1 Vixen and I couldn't have done it without my good friend Ru Barard who not only supported me on many practical levels but kept me on track to write this cracking novel and create the V universe.

A big hand also goes to Gooch Barard for his fantastic front cover photography work.

Thank you also to everyone for all their opinions and support through what can be a creatively powerful though physically draining experience of writing a novel. Especially to my wife Emilia who I love so much.

Last but certainly not least, thank-you to you the reader for buying this book. I do hope you enjoy it as much as I enjoyed writing it after an author might write a story but it is the imagination and support of readers that make it come to life.

Chapter 1

"Who's used all of the butter?" Ru asked with all the indignation that she could muster at 7 am in the morning?

There was no answer from Steve, who was sitting eating his Weetabix on the sofa while watching TV.

"Hello!" Ru shouted while holding her dry toast infant of Steve's eyes.

"Not for me thanks", he innocently blurted.

"I wasn't offering you any. I said where is my butter?" Ru repeated.

Steve stopped eating, he didn't have much choice as Ru strode over and shoved the toast between his bowl and his mouth.

"I think Mikey took it last night. I think he took the milk too. Your stuff isn't even real butter," Steve answered back.

"I know, that's my vegan stash! Your butter is still here, my fake stuff is gone. Can't you guys read 'dairy free' jeez! Fine I'll put some marmalade on it", said Ru as she turned back so suddenly her long black hair flicked out into Steve's face.

Ru was already running late for her shift and she could have done without having to rifle through the fridge looking for something to spread on her toast.

"So you ready for the party tonight?" Steve shouted over the top of the TV rather than turning the volume down.

"You know Weetabix without milk isn't as bad as you'd imagine… it's actually much worse," he continued.

Finally, Ru found the marmalade and plunged the knife deep into the jar bring out enough marmalade to almost smother the entire slice of toast. Just as she was sitting down to eat, she heard a key in the front door. After a moment, Mikey appeared holding non-dairy butter and milk aloft in both hands as if he was holding aloft a prize animal after a hunt.

"I heard you dissing me from across the hallway," he laughed.

Ruby bit into her toast, taking care not to spill any marmalade over her brilliant white pharmacy uniform.

"Dissing is when you are badmouthing someone unfairly Michael, there was nothing unfair about what I said", retorted Ru.

Mikey smiled as Ru was the only one who would call him Michael when she was mad, even though his actual name was Mike and not Michael. He wandered over and sat on the arm of the sofa so that he could be close to both Steve on the sofa and Ru, who was sat at the table.

"So you ready for your party?" Ru asked?

"Yeah man, the big 3-0 innit. Well minus a year."

Mikey reached into his pockets and pulled out a set of car keys that he chucked onto Steve's lap.

"Cheers for the car bro, I appreciate that," Mikey said in his usual Cockney-Nigerian droll.

"Is everything ok Mikey?" Ru asked?

"It's coolio, I spoke to my boss like and he's gonna give me some drinks from the bar for this evening", Mikey replied.

"No, I didn't mean that. You've been a bit stressed out all week, is everything ok?"

Mikey put his head in his hands before running his fingers through his hair.

"Oh, that. Yeah, I had a bit of a problem but it's sorted now. Just if anyone asks about me, just don't tell them anything. Not that anyone is going to like", Mikey insisted.

"You're going to get yourself in trouble one day mate," said Steve, his voice quavering from trying to hold back a cough having got one too many cardboard like dry flakes of Weetabix stuck in his throat.

"Listen, I'd love to stand here chatting all day but I gotta get to work. I'll see you later yeah?"

Ru spoke more like a general announcement than to either of the guys in particular. It was a neat arrangement, sharing a flat with Steve although she saw Mikey almost as much and he lived across the hallway in the neighbouring flat.

Ru took one last swig of her tea, grabbed her car keys from the table and opened the door. She was in such a hurry that she was halfway down the stairs before she heard the guys shout their goodbyes.

It was a typical late October morning and though it was just getting light, the air was heavy and damp from a persistent light drizzle. It was enough to make Ru hurry across to her car. She wasn't so bothered about getting wet but rather didn't want her hair to frizz from the moisture in the air.

She pressed the unlock button on her car key and the indicator lights flashed in acknowledgement that the doors were unlocked. Ru loved her car, it wasn't brand new but that wasn't important. What was important was that it was a hot looking black Audi A3 sports turbo. Ru got into her car and turned the key in the ignition which made the engine roar to life. She had the baddest car in the whole of the pharmacy department and she knew a few people wondered how she could afford to buy it but then they didn't know all the times she had to teach Jujitsu and fit in some beauty therapy at the gym in the evening when like everyone else, she just wanted to go home for a pizza and Netflix.

It was a short drive into work, the traffic this early on was never that bad unless there had been a prang at Bushey Arches or the river had burst its banks, which to Ru seemed to happen with increasing regularity. The ease of the commute was actually one of the best parts of the job. That and the late shift when there was hardly anyone around.

"Another day, another dollar" Ru sighed as she parked up in the staff section of the carpark near the side entrance to the Watford superstore before hurrying into the building. It was going to be a long day. Actually, every day was a long day but today especially what with it being Mikey's birthday get-together in the evening.

"Morning gorgeous!"

Ru smiled and looked round to see Hope the security guard waving at her. Though compliments were always nice, Hope called everyone gorgeous whether it was her, old Brenda who was in her 70's or even Dave in the stores with his bad dress sense, steel toe-capped shoes and unkempt beard that gave him a passing resemblance to the Abominable Snowman after coming out of the chiller unit. Hope always thought Ru strutted into the place like a wannabe kick-ass model but in truth, it was just Ru being Ru.

On her way into the store, Ru grew frustrated by the constant pings on her iPhone due to the stores wifi kicking in and she nearly walked into a customer trolley in the panic of rushing in to swipe in on her shift on time.

Ru put on her public smiling face, held in her stomach a bit, hoping the zipper on her uniform wouldn't snap open and walked through fruit and vegetable section, past the deodorants and makeup to her home away from home these last six years, the branch pharmacy counter. Ru tried to sound as upbeat and energetic as possible when her manager, the chief pharmacist peered up from her work as she came behind the counter.

"Morning Nads", Ru glowed.

"Hi Ru, how's things?" she asked.

Nadine was a young fashionable lady, who had recently got married in the beautiful location of Santorini, Greece. Ru had a great working relationship with her and could have easily adopted her as her sister. It was entirely possible that some of their younger male customers didn't mind waiting for their medication to be prepared too much as most would likely think Nads was pretty looking. The older ones and these were often the majority, often couldn't see or hear that well to know what was being said to them or who was saying it.

"Not bad thanks. I'll make a start on the prescriptions if there is nothing urgent needs doing?" Ru replied.

Working in a supermarket pharmacy could be an interesting job. There were all sorts of customers both good and bad and a lot of the work was varied though frequently dull. From time to time life would brighten up when the department took part in centrally organised promotions such as Health checks or anti-smoking campaigns but generally Ru found herself rather on the boring side of life unless something brightened up her day.
    Her feet often got sore from standing upright for the

length of the shifts and she sometimes felt exhausted by the end of the day, not just from the physical tiredness but the mental exhaustion too. Going through the entire prescriptions of an old people's home wasn't anyone's idea of fun and it required an incredible eye for detail. Still, Ru hadn't killed anyone yet or if she had, no-one has traced it back to her.

Generally on Friday nights, Ru looks forward to customers who purchase from the family planning section of the pharmacy on the shop floor. In particular, she knew she would need to keep a pair of long scissors nearby to wedge out condom packs from the security cases. She laughed to herself as she remembered that it takes her quite a bit of time to do this whilst knowing that customers would rather it be a quick transaction to avoid the embarrassment and wait from putting them off their mood.

Ru set about checking in the medications that had arrived overnight and preparing those that were required for the regular prescriptions that would be collected later in the day. Throughout the morning, there was a smattering of customers that Ru gave advice to in her own cheery way. Not everyone always responded well to her chirpy demeanour but Ru thought it better to be cheerful when dealing with people unwell or in distress than coming over as miserable and unfriendly.

It was an unremarkable morning, a few people coming in for cold remedies, and an old lady wanting to know whether there was anything that could be done to help her rheumatism which was keeping her awake at night whilst her husband was insistent that Ru looked the spitting image of his grand-daughter.

It seemed unlikely though as both of the old couple were very pale skinned and white and while if anyone asked Ru where she was from, she could truthfully say she was from Wolverhampton. Her family originated in India where there were very few people with as blonde hair as that of the girl in the photo that the old man was showing her. Ru wondered if it was because she defines herself as a bit of 'coconut', brown on the outside but very white British on the inside.

Ru always thought that the fact that she has lost her Black Country accent to be a blessing as she knew for a fact that many customers wouldn't understand her otherwise. Sometimes though her original accent would resurface, embarrassingly as it normally happened during her routine store tannoy announcements to promote the Pharmacy Services.

Still, Ru thought to herself, not as embarrassing as the young woman wanting a second opinion on an insect bite mark somewhere below the waist or the young guy who came in every Friday offering to marry her without the need for a Viagra prescription. That was just the most hilarious thing ever, Ru thought, especially for the 40th time, NOT.

Despite it not always being the most exciting of jobs, it was always a very tiring one. The hours were long and the shifts were at various times of day and as the work was quite trying, there was quite a high absenteeism rate meaning that Ru was often called upon to work extra shifts. She had a feeling that the company were taking the piss with her salary but she wasn't quite sure what to do about it and until her lunch break, she passed the time serving customers and wondering whether she should go back into the personal training and martial arts tutoring that she used to do.

Once Nadine had gone for her legally required break, Ru was in charge for 45 minutes but it was relatively quiet and so Ru took the time to top up the stock and check on any electronic prescriptions to be downloaded whilst waiting for her own lunch.

Lunch, when it came, was usually a simple affair either eating back in her car or eating on the go whilst she did a bit of shopping of her own whilst making the most of her staff discount. Whether it was food, household items or her hair-straightener, not much escaped her clutches with the encyclopaedic knowledge of the superstore that could only come with experience.

Sometimes she would shop for Steve too. She liked sharing the flat with him and they would have a right good laugh sometimes. Ru would often take care of the shopping whilst as Steve worked from home, he would do most of the chores. She imagined he would be getting the place all ready for Mikey right this minute. Not that it would be a big bash, just a few friends, drinks and takeaways. Ru had lived with Steve for about two years now which was 18 months longer than she had known Mikey.
Thinking about Mikey brought a smile to her face which in turned forced Ru to make a quick diversion down aisle 19

as for a split second a young man in front of her thought that the smile might have been for him. Thinking about it, she didn't believe that she could live with Mikey for two years as he was a bit crazy. Fun but crazy and she knew that Steve felt the same and that it would be nice to have him round just a little less often. I mean, his flat was only a few feet away from theirs. He was what Ru thought might be called a 'loveable rogue', a kind of Nigerian Del Boy but without the smarter brother unless the smarter brother was Steve.

With her shopping finished, she went to see Claire on the till and the pair chatted, well if truth be told, maybe gossiped might be a more accurate term. Claire was a nice girl who worked part-time whilst her kids were at school. By all accounts, her ex-boyfriend was a bit of an arse and sometimes he would even sneak into the superstore if Security was busy and make life difficult for her. Ru had taught Claire some self-defence moves which had earned her Claire's admiration and they'd become good workplace buddies.

Once the bags had been dumped in the car boot and Ru had exchanged a quick chat with Hope, she was back at her post for a few more hours. She did her best to dream the day away until a little flurry of customers just before 4 pm made her shift finish a bit busier than anticipated but they were all discerning customers and they didn't mind queuing for a few minutes.

Finally, it was home time and Ru said her good-byes as Julia came in to cover the next shift. Ru hurried through the store, barely stopping to speak to Hope. It was a Friday night after all!

"Hurray" Ru shouted to herself. Not just because it was Friday but because the drizzle had cleared. She checked the time on her mobile phone and worked out that she had time to go for a quick work-out at the gym before returning home. The air was cold enough that none of the food would go bad in the car boot, not that there was much to go bad.

She put on some 'Thirty Seconds To Mars' on the radio and as Jared strutted his stuff, Ru drove the short distance to The Country Club gym to strut hers. It was dark when she got there but she managed to park in her favourite spot, just to the right of the entrance. Her car was here almost as often as at work. Pulling out her Adidas branded gym clothes from the back seat, she was soon changed and putting her work frustrations against the rowing, cross-body trainer and weights in quick succession.

As Ru worked through the training session as she always did, keeping a focuses but steady pace whilst thinking about the evening to come with Mikey.

Ru was never one to let sweating and being out of breath deter her from hard work and the results were clear with a washboard stomach, legs with better definition than the average HD television and arms that could more than keep her out of trouble. Ru never wanted to be very muscly, just toned and in fact despite all the visible evidence to the contrary, she was very modest about her body, shy even and this made her still very approachable in the gym though like anywhere there were always the odd jealous comments from some women. There was also the occasional smarmy innuendo from a teenage boy but she wasn't shy about having a go back, besides which Ru knew that with her combat training she could beat them without barely breaking a sweat.

20km on the exercise bike though did have Ru sweating and she noticed that time had rather got away from her so she decided to call it a day. She decided to shower at home, seeing as though she would have to get changed again into her party outfit and so went back to her car.

As she walked out through Reception she sent over to the receptionist who was reading her horoscopes.

"Can I have a look at mine?" Ru asked.

"Sure, be my guest", said the receptionist, handing over the magazine to Ru.

Ru looked down the page to Scorpio, 'This could prove to be a very busy month, Scorpio. Someone close to you might come to you for help or you might just feel like helping out. This might take up more time than you'd planned for, but you'll enjoy helping your friend. Unexpectedly this might even lead to a career change. Either way, you should finish the month better than how you start it and you may learn a lesson or two along the way.'

Ru smiled and said thanks to the lady at reception. Ru loved her horoscopes and she wondered just how much of it would come true this month.

"Damn it's cold outside," said Ru as she looked for her car keys amongst the pile of clothes and towels that she had scooped from her gym locker. Finally finding it, she unlocked the car and jumped in. The engine purred to life and Ru put the heating on to the max whilst the windscreen de-misted. She doubted whether the car would be warm before she got back home so she drove back as quick as she could.

As it happened, there was quite a bit of traffic on the High Street which slowed down Ru for the first time all day and allowed her to warm herself just before she parked up for the night. She felt quite knackered and in truth could have done without entertaining tonight but she still managed to bound up the stairs to the first floor when there was a loud clatter and Ru fell over something on the landing.

"What the hell! Why did someone leave this here?" she shouted as the flat door opened with Steve looking gingerly outside.

"Is that you Ru?" he asked.

Ru dusted herself down and picked up her keys and gym kit which had gone flying across the floor.

"I wish the landlord would hurry up and get the lights sorted out here, it's been like this for 3 weeks now", Ru said as calmly as she could.

Steve ushered Ru in through the doorway before going out to see what it was that Ru had tripped over and he soon returned with a box of beers, wines and other alcoholic drinks.

"It must have been Mikey, at least, these are his drinks".

Ru was already at the kitchen sink and downing a large glass of cold water so was momentarily unable to respond as her mouth was full.

"Strange" Steve mused before continuing.

"He should have been back an hour or more ago. Why would he leave the drinks here?"

"Who knows? It's Mikey... he probably forgot to pay the pub for them, if he was paying them anything", Ru finally replied as she wiped the excess water from her lips with the back of her hand.

"Why don't you go and check if he is in his flat while I'll go and have a shower and change into something less sweaty?" Ru suggested.

Steve nodded and took his front door keys whilst Ru went into the bathroom to take a long and much deserved shower. She closed her eyes as the hot water gushed down on her, she always had her showers hot so that the room filled with steam almost like a sauna or at least what Ru imagined a sauna to be like seeing as she had never been to one.

When she was finally both clean and relaxed, she switched off the shower and wrapped herself in two towels before running along the corridor to her bedroom. She just about heard Steve say something about Mikey not being in his flat above the roar of the blow dryer but she couldn't be bothered to come out and chat until she had got ready.

As it was an informal and small party, Ru wanted something a bit low-key when choosing her outfit and she opted for some tight dark blue jeans with short black boots and a red top to match her lipstick. Mikey always liked her red top. She heard the doorbell ring while she was straightening her hair.

"Mr Mikey, you and I are going to have words one day. I hope I haven't got a bruise on my legs from you" she muttered under her breath.

Once dressed, she double checked that her eyebrows were ok in the mirror. Considering she'd been at work all day and been to the gym, she thought that she didn't look that bad and went out to the open plan kitchen and living area.

Mikey was nowhere to be seen but there were already three friends who had arrived, one of whom, Nige, let out a wolf-whistle.

"Someone has scrubbed up well tonight", he said as the others turned round to greet Ru in a more polite fashion.

"So where is the birthday boy?" asked Nige after Ru had greeted Mikey's other two friends.

"I don't know," she said as the doorbell rang. Steve switched on the music system and dashed over to the door.

"I expect this is him now…. or not" as Steve opened the door to reveal Dan and Kirstie.

"Hi guys, come on in!" Ru waved from the kitchen as she poured out some drinks.

"I'm afraid we don't know where Mikey is at the moment. For some reason, he left the drinks outside the door but didn't actually make it inside".

"His loss," said Nige as he bypassed one of Ru's freshly poured glasses of wine and ripped open a can of beer.

With everyone here except the birthday boy and with Mikey not answering his mobile, the party never really took off. Everyone chatted politely, Steve's nibbles went down well and Ru tried to spend as much time chatting to Dan and Robyn rather than Nige who as he had increasing amounts to drink, turned a bit too much of a lech for Ru's liking. As opposed to Robyn who was such a nice girl and both Steve and Ru thought she was by far the nicest person Mikey had ever introduced them to.

By about 11 pm though it was clear that Mikey wasn't going to turn up or as Nige had said at least six times "that boy would be late for his own funeral". As the guests were all Mikey's friends rather than Ru or Steve's, there wasn't that much to talk about and around about midnight Nige struck up the idea for them to go and see if Mike might be at the pub even though Steve had already checked to see that he hadn't been called in to work after all.

Ru made her legitimate excuse that she had to be in work at 8 am in the morning. Steve had no such excuse but sheepishly claimed that someone should stay here for when Mikey came home and exhaled a deep breath when he finally managed to close the door on Nige. At last, the apartment was quiet and empty except for a number of bottles on the breakfast bar and some party decorations hanging dejectedly around the living room and kitchen.

"Ugggh, that man!" screamed Ru.

"Who, Nige or Mikey? Both I guess," Steve smiled before continuing.

"I wonder where he is, though? Maybe I should go for a walk and see if I can find him, knowing him he is probably in a club somewhere smoking dope".

Ru picked up a number of bottles from around the kitchen and dropped them in the bin.

"Don't go, Steve, He could be anywhere. Listen, I've got to catch some sleep. Why don't you stay up for another hour or so and see if he comes back to his flat? We can't do much else at this time." said Ru.

Steve nodded his head in agreement.

"Night-night Ru".

"Later's Bro".

Ru closed her bedroom door and hurriedly undressed before jumping straight into bed. It had been a long day she could hear poor Steve was tidying the place up rather than leave it for the morning. She didn't know where Mikey was and worries that he was ok were generally overwhelmed by negative thoughts at messing up everyone's evening.

Ru closed her eyes and quickly went to sleep.

Chapter 2

Ru was awoken from her sleep by the sound of her phone alarm going off. 7 am on a Saturday morning was an unholy hour to get up and go to work, she thought. It was barely light outside and her throat felt dry a little sore, probably from the night before.

It was only then that she remembered that Mikey hadn't shown up for his own party. He sure had some explaining to do but not quite so much as might have been the case. Ru bent over to touch her shin. There was no bruising or swelling from when she had tripped up over the box of drinks.

"That's one thing at least," she sighed.

Running a little late, she reasoned that her shower less than 12 hours ago would see her through her morning shift at work and so got dressed. One good thing about wearing a white pharmacy jacket was that she didn't have to give too much thought as to what she was wearing underneath it, which at times like this was a saving grace.

Ru opened her bedroom door and went through to the kitchen. Steve had thoroughly cleaned up last night and the whole apartment seemed spotless. As she went to the fridge to get some milk for her cereals she noticed a post-it note stuck to the fridge door. It was from Steve, 'Stayed up till 2 am but not heard anything from Mikey. Ps you looked nice last night x'.

The compliment brought a smile to her lips even at this hour. Steve was such a good flatmate and a sweet guy and she thought of this whilst she waited for her microwaved Weetabix and milk to warm up in the microwave.

"I'm sure Mikey will turn up when he's good and ready. It is Mikey after all," Ru whispered to herself.

She ate her breakfast eaten in silence while checking the emails on her phone. Dumping her cereal bowl in the base of the sink, Ru grabbed her car keys and quietly sneaked out onto the landing, taking care not to make a sound as she closed the door. A quick glance through Mikey's letterbox revealed he was either asleep or not at home.

"What a loser!"

Ru shook her head and went off to work.

* * *

Steve switched on his iMac and went to make another cup of tea. Switching on his old PC used to mean having enough time to go to the toilet, make some tea and possibly wait for the washing machine to go through an entire wash cycle before it booted up. His new iMac though came out of sleep mode in half a second, if that. It's increased efficiency was usually laudable but at times when he wasn't feeling efficient, it almost made him feel pressured or inadequate as if he had to work harder and faster to keep it happy.

Returning to the table with a cuppa in one hand and a biscuit in the other he decided to buy himself time by texting Mikey but like the others he had sent in the last 12 hours, he didn't receive a read-receipt. Steve wasn't the sort of person to get overly worried about much. He was every bit the laid back writer that his carefree image portrayed but there was something at the back of his mind that made him wonder if he could call the police. Did anyone else care about Mikey enough to call 999 themselves? If he wasn't going to do it now, what would change in 10 hours time or 10 days come to that. The truth was that no-one really knew much about Mikey, despite his gregarious gangsta image.

Steve started dialing in 999 but stopped after the second digit.
"It's no use, though, they wouldn't even log a call if it's less than 24 hours and let's face it Mikey has disappeared for longer than that before," he surmised.

Steve forced a smile when he remembered hearing from a mutual friend that Mikey once disappeared for three weeks and no-one ever knew where he had gone to. The word on the street was he was in jail; others said he was detained in Nigeria or that he was in hiding but from whom, no-one knew. Steve just thought it was typical Mikey.

"Now back to work Stevey boy", he muttered to himself as he got back to his writing. He knew he shouldn't moan as freelancing from home was a dream. He had the most comfortable office imaginable and no manager, the only downsides were the pay or lack of it and that somehow despite all logic, his hours working for himself at home were longer than most of those who actually went to work. He always hated going to work and knew he was uniquely disciplined that he could do his work totally without supervision or without managers less capable than himself, screwing things up with their emails, pressure and lack of organisation and planning.

It was a nicely decorated new-build apartment, all recess lights and laminate flooring, in a small block just off Bushey High Street, there was generally no crime around that he had noticed and the whole neighbourhood was nice and quiet which is what Steve generally needed when he did his writing. The countryside was just round the corner but then 30 minutes on the Jubilee Line and he could be in central London which made things easy when he had to go and meet with clients.

He had already written several short pieces this morning and was waiting on a delivery so that he could write a new product review. It was proving to be a very varied day as he had already written on 'Things to do in Edinburgh', the legendary crime matriarch of Melbourne, Kath Pettingill and some bizarre sounding and perhaps slightly dubious health supplement called 'Black Ant'. Still as long as they paid up, Steve didn't really care what it was he was writing about.

He was just about to take a bite out of his biscuit when there was a knock at the door.

"How timely", he smiled as he went to answer it.

Steve presumed it must be his delivery seeing as they never really had visitors and if it were Mikey then he would just let himself in. Before he even reached the door, there was another knock.

"You're keen!" he said when opening the door. To his surprise, though, there was so no delivery man at all. Instead, before the door was even fully opened three men barged their way in nearly hitting the door in Steve's face.

"What the hell are you doing man?"

"Shut it!"

A tall slim black guy sporting a shaved head and goatee beard lunged forward and grabbed him by the neck and pushed him firmly back against the wall whilst an Asian pulled out a butterfly knife and held it to Steve's right cheek.

"I don't want any trouble, take whatever you want."

"It's a bit too late for that my man."

Steve's eyes darted from side to side, he was looking to see if there was anything he could grab but all the knives were over in the kitchen and there wasn't even a loaf of bread to swing at his attackers, not that bread would be much use against a man with a knife at his throat. Instead, he squirmed in a vain attempt to loosen the man's grip around his neck

"Is this about Mikey?" Steve asked whilst trying not to sound like he was going to wet his pants.

"Yeah it's about Mikey", the man wielding the knife spat back.

"Quiet Dinesh, I'll do the talking round here" the third man in the group of three ordered. He was a big blonde white man in his early 40's. More overweight than muscular but despite this, he gave Steve the general impression that he was not to be messed with.

"My name's Ivo, I'm a friend of Mikey's. What do you know about him?" the leader asked?

"Nothing, I haven't even seen him for over a day. The idiot didn't even turn up for his own birthday party".

Steve raised his hands up slowly in an attempt to appear non-confrontational.

"Any chance you can get him to loosen his grip?" Steve nodded towards the man who had him pinned to the wall.

The boss seemed to both shake and nod his head, a split second later the man released his grip only to punch Steve in the stomach. Steve was taken entirely by surprise and the pain came a distinct second to the shock he felt as he doubled up as he tried but failed to catch his breath.

"Listen, now that we've your attention. Mikey has something of ours and we want it back," Ivo insisted.

Steve looked up at his interrogator and with some effort asked what it was exactly that Mikey had of theirs.

"Never mind what it is," smirked the boss.

"Omar, Dinesh, have a look around. See if you can find it" he barked.

Steve took a deep breath. Even though he was still in a compromised situation, he felt infinitely more at ease after being released. Dinesh was musclebound from head to toe, even his leather jacket looked like it sported muscles. If it were possible to have muscly ankles, then Dinesh would be the one to have them. Omar, on the other hand, was as lanky as they come. Steve thought he could be Ethiopian or maybe from Somalia and if it weren't for the other two, he fancied his chance with him.

"You, what's your name?" Ivo asked.

"Steve", Steve replied having regained his breath and composure.

"Why don't you take a seat", the boss said as he motioned for Steve to sit on the floor at the base of the wall.

"Listen, you tell us where it is and we'll make sure nobody gets hurt," he continued.

Steve slumped at the base of the wall, his breathing became calmer as air returned once more to his lungs.

"It's hard to tell you something I don't know anything about," Steve protested.

If his voice sounded innocent then it was because Steve genuinely didn't know what Ivo was on about. If he didn't even know why Mikey had not shown up for his own birthday party then it is unlikely he would know anything else.

"Don't give me that, you must know what it is. We know Mickey spends as much time here as over in his gaffe."

"Have you had a look in his place?" Steve asked, trying anything he could think to get them to leave.

"We did, couldn't find what we were looking for, or anything else for that matter," the intruder replied.

Steve watched as Ivo and Omar opened up all the kitchen cupboards, standing on chairs to make sure they could check on top. Afterwards, they moved into the living room and tore out the cushions before upturning the sofa and chairs. Steve hoped they wouldn't smash up his iMac or the big screen tv but he needn't have worried as they didn't seem intent on destroying anything, just looking for whatever it was they were after.

"Check the bedrooms," Ivo hollered.

"You mind if I smoke?" Ivo asked Steve as his two accomplices disappeared towards the bedrooms.

Steve shook his head.

"If I had a choice I'd say no as Ru has asthma".

Ivo started laughing.

"I like your humour. I can see why Mikey likes you".

Steve sat in silence as Ivo lit a cigarette. He could hear shouting from the bedrooms, obviously, they couldn't find what they were looking for and within a few minutes, Dinesh and Omar came back to report as such.

"We didn't find nothing", Omar said

"Except some cute outfits in the girls room," Dinesh countered.

Ivo took a deep drag on his cigarette before exhaling slowly.

"You know what I think Steve?" Ivo asked

Steve shook his head.

"Not really no. I wish I did."

"I think that you're a nice guy but I'm not sure you know just how serious we are."

Ivo took one last smoke of his cigarette before flicking it down onto Steve with his fingers.

"You see Mikey, you make sure to tell him that The Walkers are looking for him and give him this message".

"Sure what?" asked Steve.

Suddenly Dinesh picked up a stool from the breakfast bar and pushed through Ivo and Dinesh and smashed it across Steve's head sending pieces flying across the floor and leaving Steve slumped sideways onto the floor. Even as a trickle of blood seeped out from a gash on his Steve's forehead, Ivo stepped forward and kicked him twice in the stomach.

"That's it, he got the message, come on boys", Ivo sniggered

The 'boys' followed Ivo through the front door and slammed it shut leaving Steve clutching at his head. For a moment he lay motionless on the laminate floor before he summoned up the energy to pull himself up, using the wall for support. He reached into his back pocket for his mobile phone, Steve felt dizzy and he staggered towards the sofa as if he were walking on the deck of a ship on hurricane strength winds. He was so unsteady on his feet that he fell sideways onto the table before grabbing hold of a chair to sit on.

He put his hand up to his head, he was bleeding but not that badly but both his head and his chest hurt like crazy. Finding Ru on his speed-dial he gave her a call but the phone rang six times before going to answerphone.

"Damn", he sighed.

Steve wondered if he should call the police or even the ambulance but in the end, the decision was made for him as a sharp pain struck through his head and he dropped the phone on the floor bouncing away out of sight. He decided to lay his head flat on the table and wait for the pain to subside.

"What the hell is going on?" he asked himself but he had no answers. Only Mikey could help but the more Steve thought about it, the more unlikely it seemed that he would see Mikey for a long time to come.

Chapter 3

There had been some sort of car crash near Bushey Arches and Ru had been stuck in the resultant traffic queues that stretched way back past the Ring Road. She'd lost her patience after the first 45 minutes of going nowhere very quickly. It had already been a bad day at work as she had been covering for a sick colleague and had been rushed off her feet by a steady flow of customers wanting advice, prescriptions, purchases or just a friendly chat.

Ru hadn't even had a chance to check her phone until she was walking out of the building at the end of her shift and it was then she saw she had got half a dozen missed calls from Steve over four hours earlier. Ru immediately knew something was wrong as Steve never ever called her, in fact, he never called anyone as he disliked using telephones. She instantly tried calling him back but his phone just rang and rang which wasn't like Steve at all. What with Mikey vanishing and Steve obviously repeatedly calling her hours ago, something major was up and the fact she didn't know what exactly put her on edge and she let half of Watford know it when she pipped her car horn in frustration. If it helped her frustration somewhat, it did little to help move the traffic in front and she was soon surrounded by a cacophony of cars also sounding their horn in annoyance leaving the whole street to sound like the worst ever orchestra performance ever.

Her 10-minute journey home had already taken more than an hour when at last the traffic began moving in a bumbling unsure and erratic way, crawling forwards a few feet only to stop for 20 seconds before repeating the process over and over. Eventually, the apprehensively moving traffic queue saw Ru finally reach the obstruction to see that three cars had collided at the Bushey Arches roundabout. The railway viaduct combined with the usual chaos of so many roads meeting together meant that the recovery operation was moving as quickly as an asthmatic snail.

Ru swore under her breath has she finally cleared the accident and moved up the hill where a set of traffic lights temporarily held her up for a few moments. Once the lights turned green there was no stopping her and she roared forwards towards home. Her heart was beating quickly and she could hear it loudly as if it were hammering inside her head. The car tyres screeched as she turned into her road at speed. As soon as she entered the communal parking area, her anxiety hardly lessened at the sight of a police car parked near to the entrance of the block of flats.

Ru's first thoughts were that it was Mikey. Had he got himself in trouble? Was he missing? To be honest Ru's mind jumped to the worst conclusion and that he might be dead. Grabbing her belongings, she pushed open the car door and closed it again with a gentle kick from her right leg and she was already at the bottom of the stairwell before she remembered to press the button on the remote to lock the car.

She ran up the stairs two, sometimes three at a time and reached the first floor with breathtaking speed.

"Oh my God!" she exclaimed.

Mikey's front door was wide open and by the light from upstairs, she could make out that much of his front room has been turned over. She took a deep breath, put her key in the lock and opened the door.

"And that's all you can say?"

"Yes, officer".

"Well, I don't think they will back here again. You really should get to A&E and get yourself checked out".

Ru closed the door quietly behind, she was shocked to see a broken chair splintered across the kitchen and a trail of blood. She hurried into the living area to see Steve sat on the sofa holding a hand towel against his head. It's natural beige colouring now supplemented by some large deep red and almost burgundy coloured blood stains.

On the other chair sat a tall, slim police officer, Ru estimated him to be in his mid 30's. His hat was perched on the arm of the chair and the officer had obviously made scrupulous notes in the A5 pad he held on his lap. Neither of them had noticed Ru's entry and she could see that aside from his obvious wounds, Steve looked both shaken up and uncomfortable with one hand holding the towel against his head and the other clutching his chest.

"Oh my God, what happened? Have you found Mikey?" her fast flowing, flustered questions catching both men by surprise.

"No, they haven't. Err, Hi Ru", Steve forced a smile.

The policeman turned in his chair to see it was who had interrupted their conversation.

"And you are Miss?"

"Ruby Barard, I'm a flatmate of Steve and Mikey. Well of Steve anyway as Miked lives over there in that smashed up flat. "

Ru went straight over to get some kitchen roll and tore off multiple sheets before dampening them under the kitchen tap and going over to Steve.

"Let me see", she said, her obvious concern coming through her voice.

"Oh my God Steve, what happened," she asked as she started wiping away blood from his head.

"I'm not really sure".

"I'm sorry Miss", the policeman appeared hesitant to interrupt.

"But have you seen Mikey in the last 48 hours".

Ru shook her head.

"No, the last time I saw him was when I left him here at breakfast yesterday morning. I tried calling him but got nowhere. I guessed that he would just turn up", she explained to the police officer whilst never diverting her attention from Steve's head.

"Do you know what's happening?" Ru asked.

"Where has Mikey gone? Who smashed up the apartments and did this to Steve?"

"I'm sorry Miss but I can't tell you anything at the time. Steve managed to give us some descriptions of the men involved but as they wore gloves there aren't any fingerprints and to be honest, they're aren't going to do a sweep for DNA evidence for this".

Ru nodded in acknowledgement.

"So we can clear up this mess then?"

The police officer put his pen and notepad in his front pocket and stood up, taking his police cap in hand.

"We'll let you know if we find anything out and in the meantime, keep everything locked. Someone will be round later to secure Mikey's flat."

The officer reached into his inside jacket pocket and pulled out a card which he gave to Ru, who read it out loud.

'Sgt John Wilkinson, Watford Police Station, Hertfordshire Constabulary.'

"Try not to worry, it's not likely they are going to come back here," the Sergeant said in his most reassuring voice.

Ru nodded her head.

"Are you going to catch them?"

"Steve here gave quite a good description so it's a good start but because they were wearing gloves and were careful. My guess is that your friend Mikey has got involved in something a bit out of his depth and he's done a runner until things calm down a bit".

Ru had already come to the same conclusions but didn't want to say anything to Sherlock.

"I'll be in touch", the sergeant said as he left the flat.

"Oh my God, Steve, what happened?"

Steve spoke while Ru continued treating his wounds. Though he felt awful, Steve suspected that he looked even worse.

"I don't know, someone was at the door. I thought it was the delivery I was waiting for and when I opened the door, these three guys barged in. They were looking for Mikey. Ow!"

Steve winced at a stabbing pain that caught him by surprise as Ru dabbed on some antiseptic cream.

"We're going to have to get you to A & E, you need stitches. Look at your face, you're black and blue". As Ru spoke, she couldn't hide the concerned look on her face.

"Anyway", Steve continued, "I told them I don't know where Mikey is and they tore up the flat while one of them decked me and held me at knife point. When they couldn't find anything they smashed a chair on me and then started kicking at me on the floor".

"I'm so sorry Steve."

"Don't be, I'm glad you weren't here. No point in us both getting beaten up".

Ru went over to the kitchen and tore off a few strips of kitchen roll.

"Maybe I could have stopped them, I know how to handle myself. Here, hold one of these on your head to slow the bleeding. I'll come with you to the hospital and I'm not taking no for an answer."

Resigned to his fate, Steve nodded his head in a painful show of agreement. He knew there was no point in disagreeing, Ru could be very forceful when she wanted to.

Ru grabbed her car keys and helped Steve out the flat and down the stairs. She realised when they were getting in the car that they had forgotten to lock the front door but she didn't bother going back, there didn't seem much point seeing the state the place was in.

"I'll try not to get too much blood on the leathers". Steve attempted to make it sound a joke but he was too sore to make it seem anything like funny.

Ru indulged him though as they set off to Watford General.

"You better not Steve, you've already lost one fight today. Don't make me deck you!"

As she knew that the traffic was bad, Ru took a detour around the houses and through the park. They still go stuck in traffic but only for the last mile or so. The pair sat in near silence as they slowly worked their way through the traffic. Ru hoped that they were still early enough to avoid the usual Friday night A&E hell with the drunks, yobs and chavs that take-over the A&E at the weekends and was pleased to see that it was comparatively quiet. Maybe everyone was stuck in traffic.

They only waited for 10 minutes before Steve was called through. Ru had got carried away playing 8 ball pool on her iPhone and did her best to continue playing as they walked to a treatment area.

The doctor was a rather strict sounding South African lady that didn't immediately grab Steve as being overly sympathetic as she examined him. Steve didn't want her to think he had been in a drunken fight especially not this early and after a few minutes decided to break the ice.

"I didn't get in a fight or anything", Steve protested.

"Really?" the doctor replied but didn't stop her work.

"Well it wasn't so much a fight as a beating…. they broke into my flat when I was working" he profused.

There was a slight pause before the doctor spoke.

"You're going to need 5 or maybe 6 stitches in your head and you're going to wake up tomorrow looking and feeling like you've been hit by a truck. We will get you X-rayed as a precaution but I think you've been lucky and there aren't any fractures."

"I don't feel very lucky", Steve sighed to himself as the doctor prepared the stitches.

"Now hold tight, this might hurt a bit."

"Yessss!" Ru exclaimed.

Both the doctor and Steve looked round.

"Sorry, not 'yes' for it hurting. I've just won in the Moscow bar in 8-ball pool".

"Did you lose consciousness at all? Have you been dizzy or vomited?" the doctor asked.

Steve sat as still as he could and shut his eyes to try and minimise the pain only to open them after the first two stitches. He could just about see Ru looking down over the doctor's shoulders.

"No, I was awake the whole time and I haven't vomited but I did feel dizzy for a few hours but that's been overtaken by a general nauseous feeling", he explained.

"That's to be expected, I'm afraid you're going to be a bit sore for several days… is this your wife?".

"Err no, this isn't his wife… just his friend and flatmate", Ru explained trying not to sound as flabbergasted as she was. "I work in the pharmacy at a big supermarket, don't worry I'll look after him".

Finally after what seemed like a never-ending period of squints, winces and involuntary teeth gritting, the doctor announced that he was all stitched up.

"Do you want to go back to the waiting area and I'll take your friend to X-Ray", the doctor ordered rather than suggested.

Ru knew when she wasn't wanted and like Steve was rather intimidated by the abrasive manner of the physician.

"I'll wait for you Steve" she smiled.

Ru watched as the doctor helped Steve down the corridor before turning back to the waiting room. She got a plastic cup of hot chocolate from the vending machine and picked the quietest section of the A&E waiting area before whipping her phone out.

"May as well play some pool while I'm here," she surmised.

As it happened Ru had more than enough time to play pool on Facebook as Steve took longer getting X-rayed than he did both for waiting at A&E and then being stitched up afterwards. As the doctor thought he had no fractures about his head but he was suffering from a broken rib and two others were bruised. By the time he had been patched up, they didn't get out of the hospital until nearly 10 pm.

Knowing the pharmacy closed at 10 even though the store itself was open until midnight, she called Nadine and arranged for some prescriptions to be readied for Steve which she collected on the way home. There was now no sign of any car crash and just a few minutes later, Steve had taken his tablets and been ushered to bed whilst Ru stayed up even later tidying the flat up. Realistically she knew it was unlikely the men would come back to the flat so she wasn't that worried about them but it made her uncomfortable having strangers going through all her stuff as she was a very private person.

When she finally went to bed, her thoughts settled on Steve, he would surely feel uncomfortable having endured such an attack in his own home. Poor chap.

The next morning both Steve and Ru were late getting up well late by normal standards. Steve generally woke between 5 am and 6 am and whether, through exhaustion or the pills he had taken, he didn't wake up until 8 am. He hurt everywhere and so hurried into the kitchen only his hurrying was about the speed of a snail and he imagined himself to resemble some beaten old age pensioner desperately seeking a fix of drugs as he swallowed them with a glass of orange juice. He was still sat clutching the glass on the sofa when Ru got up nearly an hour later.

"Did you sleep okay?" he asked her.

Ru nodded.

"I'll make some breakfast," she said as she walked over to take a look at Steve's injuries. At least, the stitches had stopped the bleeding but half of his face was swollen up and coloured a thousand shades of green, brown and red.

"You poor thing, you must be sore".

Steve didn't answer but meekly nodded his head and shrugged his shoulders in agreement. As Ru made breakfast, Steve switched on the television with the remote control.

"I have a feeling you and me are going to get well acquainted this weekend", Ru said.

"Here you go! Let me know when you want your tea and I'll get it for you."

Ru handed Steve a plate of toast.

"Remember the doctors said to rest so no going on your computer and limited TV time. You understand?"

Steve wasn't exactly feeling very ravenous at first but the more he ate, the more he wanted to eat which made sense given that he hadn't eaten for over 24 hours.

"I put a towel over the mirror in the Bathroom, do yourself a favour and don't look in the mirror".

"Do I look that bad?"

"You look awful, it hurts me just to look at you", Ru confided.

"Could I have some tea, please?" Steve asked.

Ru bent over and picked up a mug of tea from the floor.

"Thanks, Ru. My God I feel like crap."

"I can't believe someone would do this to you. No wonder Mikey is on the run… the little shit. He could have told us".

Hearing Ru swear made Steve laugh but it hurt his ribs so he stifled it as much as he could.

Ru spent all morning chilling as best as she could as Steve sat on the sofa. It hurt him to move and it hurt him to sit still so long so after lunch he took another painkiller. He'd been given tablets to help him sleep too but wasn't sure if he should take one in the day and Ru said to keep them for later.

"Do you mind if I pop out for a bit. I was thinking of going down to The Horns to see if Mikey has re-surfaced?" Ru asked.

Steve shook his head.

"No I'll be ok, I have two drinks on either side of me, some crisps, grapes and the telly. I'll be fine".

Ru went into her room and changed our of her PJ's and into something she could actually wear outside. She didn't want to look too conspicuous so just wore some tight jeans and a pair of her least high-heeled boots. The Horns was never the place to dress up to and most girls who went there would have just worn trainers but Ru did have some standards.

Ru gave Steve his mobile phone.

"Call me if you need anything and I promise I will come straight back in 5 minutes. I'll be back in an hour or two anyway".

"I will be careful," Ru said when she saw the worried look on Steve's face. At least, she thought it was a worried look, it was hard to make out with the bruisings, swellings and discolourations.

Steve reached out his hand and Ru gave it a quick squeeze as she headed out.

"Laters yeah".

"I'm not going anywhere", Steve replied.

Ru grabbed her black leather jacket and closed the door quietly on her way out. The police had obviously been and boarded up the entrance to Mickey's flat as it was securely blocked off now. Though she didn't expect to actually find Mikey at The Horns, she did hope to find out some news… any news. In truth though at the moment she wasn't doing this for Mikey but for Steve and though she didn't say much to Steve about it, Ru felt a queasy mixture of shock, disgust and anger at what this gang had done to her flat-mate whom Mikey himself always used to call his brother from another mother.

It only took a few minutes in the car to get to the pub and it was only when she parked up that Ru checked to see that Steve hadn't actually dripped any blood over her upholstery. Fortunately, he hadn't, not that she would have blamed him for any stains. She loved her car but there were limits. Ru switched off the engine and took a deep breath that turned into a long sigh. The Horns was a busy little pub and excellent live music venue some nights but it was not the sort of place Ru generally visited voluntarily. In the broad daylight, it was obviously much safer but it was also, even more evident, what a dump the whole place was. In a way if you had to pick a place that Mikey might work at then Ru thought you'd have to go a long way to beat The Horns.

Ru pulled down the vanity mirror to check how she looked, not that she had to worry about having any competition in this place. Giving herself the quick seal of approval she exited her car and walked across the littered covered carpark to the entrance where two hooded teenagers stood smoking.

"Nice legs," said one of the chavs to the other.

"Nice car," said the other to Ru as she walked past.

"Yeah, it better still be when I come back out".

"Bitch!", the chavs replied back under their breath almost in unison.

Ru didn't hear though as she was already inside. It was a dark, rundown sort of pub, the kind that oozed dirt and smoke even without any smokers. Touch anything in here and you'd want to wash your hands, Ru thought to herself. There was only a table of three men in one corner and another older bloke standing at the bar but otherwise, the place was empty and silent except for the football on the telly.

Ru walked over to the bar, her loud footsteps either ignored or unnoticed to the barman who was staring at the TV screen. It was Nev, the landlord and Mikey's boss. Ru didn't really know him well but always thought that he was well suited to the place as his jeans were normally ripped, his balding hair greasy and normally his polo shirt was beer stained. The fact that today he seemed to have a bit of dried ketchup under his chin was Ru thought, at least, a change.

"Ru...didn't expect to see you here", said Nev.

"Me neither… you seen Mikey?" she asked.

Nev shook his head.

"Between you and me, I'm not sure whether to be worried for him or angry at him for disappearing... and he didn't pay for his birthday booze", Nev said ruefully.

"Listen, Nev, our place got broken into yesterday and Steve got smashed up by three guys looking for Mikey. I need to find out where he is or at least who these guys were".

"Really! Shit no way. I'm sorry, is he okay?"

Give him his due Ru thought. Nev sounded as genuinely shocked as she could ever imagine him being.

"Have any of Mikey's mates been in?" Ru asked without mentioning Steve.

"Not seen anything from any of them but normally about 3 pm Danny turns up".

"Danny?" Ru asked.

Nev leant over the bar and lowered the tone of his voice forcing Ru to strain her ears to hear him.

"Danny is err a business associate of Mikey, sometimes they help each other out with money making opportunities if you know what I mean?" Nev widened his eyes in an exaggerated fashion that in any other situation would look like he'd just sat on a drawing pin.

It was 2.40pm now, Ru thought she could easily hang around to see if this Danny guy turned up.

"I'll go and sit over there, can you send him over if he comes in" Ru asked.

"You'll have to order a drink I'm afraid,' said Nev, always the business man.

"Oh yeah, sorry. I'll have a mineral water please" Ru replied as she reached into her bag for her purse.

"No I mean a real drink", Nev tutted.
"I don't drink alcohol", Ru insisted.

"Danny won't speak to you if you're not drinking".

"Why not?"

"He doesn't trust people who don't drink. If he doesn't trust you then, he's not likely to help you, even looking like you do Ru."

"Fine, I'll have a white wine… no, half a pint. I don't mind what of. I might as well be convincing".

Ru watched Nev pour out a lager.

"That'll be £1.90 please Ru".

Ru handed over the money and walked over to the furthest and dingiest corner of the bar and waited. Just as Nev had advised, a scrawny guy with pierced ears and the shiniest shell suit this side of the 1980's came in soon after 3 pm. Ru watched as he went over to order a drink and Nev pointed her out.

Ru took a sip of her lager, she thought she may as well, rather than just sitting watching the bubbles as that was hardly likely to get Danny to talk. After a few seconds, Danny came over with a fully laden pint glass in one hand and his mobile and car keys on the other.

"You're Mikey's roomie?" Danny asked as he noisily pulled out a wooden chair, scraping it on the dirty looking floor as he did so.

"Well, I live opposite him. Can you tell me where he is? Three guys came round looking for him yesterday and smashed my place up and left my mate with stitches and a broken rib".

Ru took another but a bigger sip of her lager and tried to swallow it without pulling a face of disgust.

"Sorry Ru. I don't know where he is, I came here incase he turned up. I do know he was involved with something dodgy." Danny replied.

"What sort of dodgy"? Ru asked.

"Drugs if I know Mikey. I think he was a bit out of his depth if you ask me".

"I can see why Mikey talked about you a lot, what you doing later Ru?"

Ru moved uncomfortably in her seat, it was bad enough being hit on by a sleazeball, let alone a drug dealer. She took another mouthful of drink and felt the bubble go up her nose before replying.

"Sorry got to look after my flatmate. Maybe next time yeah".

Surprisingly to Ru, Danny didn't seem at all shocked or disappointed by her limp but hopefully plausible refusal.

"These guys who smashed up your place. I went with Mikey to see them a few months ago, not to do with this but some other job. Anyway, you might want to check them out as they used to work out of an old warehouse in South Ruislip. Stone Field Way, corner of Stonefield Close. If they aren't there, then often they can be seen at Diamonds, you know the club on the west side of town with that live stage and hotel at the back... they are there quite often in the evenings not that Mikey would be there. A bit too polished for him innit."

"Seriously?" said Ru, not expecting Danny to be anything like so forthcoming.

Danny nodded his head.

"Keep it low profile you know. You didn't see me, you understand" Danny said, his voice lowering into a gravelly tone and for the first time coming over as the menacing person Ru imagined he so easily could be.

"Don't involve the Feds either, not if you know what's good for you, Mikey or your flatmate."

Ru took her biggest mouthful of lager yet.

"Don't worry, I'm not stupid". Ru insisted.

"Listen, my partners just come in so I've got stuff to sort out. Be careful yeah".

Danny motioned his head over to two guys who had just walked in and Ru thought they looked like trouble. Ru felt like she needed a drink. She hadn't known that feeling before. Usually, she felt like she needed to go to the gym or lay into someone in the self-defence courses. Ru drank a bit more of her drink.

"I've got to get back to Steve," she said as she pulled her chair away from the table.

"Thanks, Danny".

A thousand thoughts were running through Ru's head. Should she tell the police? Maybe go to this warehouse now? She marched out to the door pushing right past Danny's partners, one of whom turned and leered at her.

"No, be realistic Ru. You can't do this on your own without thinking. Maybe Steve will have an idea", she murmured to herself.

Back out in the daylight, she was relieved to see her car was still in one piece but her mind was racing all over the place.

"Damn", she said as she started the car and headed back home.

Chapter 4

Ru hadn't got much sleep last night but was still all ready to head off to the gym at 7 am before remembering that it was a Sunday so it wouldn't be open until 8 am. To pass the time, she went for a 5-mile run and then, feeling like she was still bursting with energy, headed off to the gym to take out her frustration on the weights. At this time on a Sunday morning, she had the place to herself and an hour later she finally headed back home. It was a sunny autumnal morning and the leaves were looking spectacular both those still on the trees and those that had fallen to the ground and created crisp golden piles that the wind had blown up across the pavement against the fences that she drove past.

Ru had an ache in her stomach and it wasn't from her Abs training. Having talked things through with Steve last night, she knew that today was going to be a big day. After much debate, a Balti delivery and more discussion they'd decided that they were going to follow the tip-off that Ru had got from Mikey's old stomping ground.

Both Ru and Steve had thought to call the police but they didn't want to involve them until they had more facts. The last thing Mikey or indeed Steve needed was the gang get twitchy about the police sniffing around. Still, though it seemed kind of stupid to Ru, it was also somehow very exciting which is no doubt why she had butterflies.

Steve was just getting up when Ru got back. His head wound where the stitches were inserted was beginning to heal but a large section of his face was a dark reddish purple and it was still puffed up like a poisonous tropical blowfish. Though no longer dizzy or disorientated when standing up, he felt in constant pain from his broken ribs and bruising. In fact, it hurt every time he took a breath or let out a cough or even changing position on the sofa. Walking was something that required concentration and if he moved to quickly he would emit a rather pitiful yelp of pain much like a dog whose paw had accidentally been trodden on.

"Morning Ru, you been out running?" Steve asked.

"I did earlier but then I went to the gym for a bit. Do you want some breakfast?"

"Beans on toast would be fab," Steve said before hobbling over to put the kettle on.

"Are you sure this is the right thing to do Ru?"

"No…. you?" Ru replied.

Steve shook his head.

"Let's go straight after breakfast" Ru suggested.

"Good plan Ru, they'll all be at church on a Sunday morning" Steve joked.

It was a tense, nervy breakfast and neither Ru or Steve really said a word to each other and instead focused on watching the repeat of WWE Smackdown. After a while,

Steve went back to his room to get changed while Ru was content to wear her gym kit albeit with a hoodie on top as it was a bit chilly outside.

"Do you think we need these?" Steve asked from his room before appearing in the lounge holding a cricket bat and two balaclavas aloft in his hands.

Ru giggled.

"Not unless you need it as a walking stick. We can take the wooly ski-masks though just in case we need to keep a low profile." Ru agreed.

"We can go in my car if you don't mind driving?" Steve suggested.

"A slightly battered Kia might look more the part in an industrial estate than your flashy Audi", Steve remarked convincingly.

It seemed to make sense to Ru and having double checked the building on Google street-view, they switched off the TV and locked the front door behind them. Stairs weren't the easiest things for Steve to negotiate and Ru teased him that it might be quicker if they installed a pole to slide down or even that she should carry him down the stairs instead.

"Do that and everyone will think you did this to me instead of them", he answered her right back in his usual trademark quick-witted style.

Steve's silver Kia had quite a few leaves and clumps of moss laying on his car windscreen which had to be moved before they could drive off. He didn't use his car much and instead preferred his bike. They couldn't do much about the white streaks on the car from the birds that gave the impression they had used his car as target practice for a sustained period of time.

"Maybe I just need to wash it a bit more often," he said to himself as Ru started the engine.

Ru drove slowly down the residential streets taking care with the speed bumps in case they jarred Steve too much and when they were out into passes for the open road she hit the play button on the car's CD player. To her surprise, the speakers were blaring out some heavy-metal music.

It's all about the game and how you play it.
All about control and if you can take it.
All about your debt and if you can pay it.
It's all about pain and who's gonna make it.

"I thought you liked the classical stuff, Steve?" Ru asked as she fumbled to lower the volume she accidentally switched it off completely.

"That my dear Ru is a classic, The Game by Motorhead."

"I meant like Beethoven or Mozart," said Ru.

Steve leant over and pressed a button on the radio and ClassicFM on.

"Better?", he asked.

Ru nodded in agreement while making a mental note to borrow the CD for her car. She didn't know Steve liked that sort of music but she wondered why not as he had all kinds of music on his iTunes, some of it was bound to be good.

The drive to the industrial estate took about 20 minutes and for half of that, they listened to the Crown Imperial by William Walton, which helped put their nerves a little at ease. Eventually after a series of turns they left the leafy suburbs and entered an industrial estate. The road was heavily potholed and the place was full of litter. It seemed that they were the only vehicle on the roads. If so, it would make little difference that Ru switched off the radio but she did so anyway so that they didn't draw undue attention to themselves as they drove past on a reconnaissance.

Ru had no problem identifying the precise location as it was the most imposing building for several hundred metres, a large double storey warehouse with a brick front reception but otherwise seemingly enclosed by metal sheeting on the walls and roof. Even from the quick drive-by, it was clear that the place was not being used, at least not by any legitimate business. The windows were whited out and tall weeds were growing up in the carpark and everything looked well and truly locked up and closed down.

Ru parked the car about 100 metres up the road behind a wall of a neighbouring property that looked almost as derelict as the warehouse. Neither Ru or Steve knew exactly what the plan was which lead both to conclude that there was no real plan at all beyond winging it. Besides which, it was quite possible that the tip-off was entirely erroneous or that the information was out of date and the gang had moved on.

"Let's take a look around. Maybe we'll find what we're looking for and we'll take it from there" she said.

Steve frowned.

"Or not," he suggested.

They got out of the car and Ru tried to press the locking button on the keyfob but couldn't find it.

"Don't bother, it doesn't have remote locking. May as well keep it unlocked in case we have to do a runner quickly like" Steve advised.

It made sense to Ru and so rather like amateurish bank robbers on their first job, they put their black balaclavas over their heads as they walked as casually as they could towards the warehouse. The building seemed to be surrounded on all sides by a two-metre security fence with jagged spikes on the top which Ru thought would be more than enough to keep Steve out given his condition. Instead, they walked round the back, passing three slightly battered looking industrial sized wheelie bins that were by the roadside.

Ru's hunch was right, druggies would be no more happy about scaling a fierce two-metre high fence than anyone else and round the back, two of the steel fencing posts had been bent out of shape creating a gap just big enough for someone to squeeze through. Ru looked around carefully but couldn't see or hear anything out of the norm and so squeezed through the gap in the fence with Steve following a few seconds later having mentally prepared himself for the inevitable pain as he squeezed between the steel fencing.

The warehouse was constructed from some sort of reinforced aluminium sheeting with an overgrown paved path running around its perimeter. Here and there were old card box boxes and scrap metal and Ru dreaded that they might accidentally trip up over something in the undergrowth that alerted those inside to their presence.

It took a few minutes to find a way into the building as the two doors on the side of the building were of no use. One was a fire door and unable to open from the outside while the other door was blocked by lots of racking. After a brief search, Steve found a small section of aluminium sheeting that had come loose near the ground which with a bit of effort they managed to squeeze through on their hands and knees.

It was dark and grimy inside. The floor seemed to be dusty and gritty with some old oil stains scattered around and Steve thought it must have been a heavy industrial plant of some sort in its previous incarnation. They had emerged into a small corner of the warehouse that was rather compartmentalised from the rest of the interior, with blocks of metal shelving stretching up seven or eight feet up towards and the corrugated steel roof that stood high above.

Ru peered through the shelving, there seemed to be lots more zones of shelving running off to the distance while, in another area, some welding machines and some sort of industrial grinder or cutter sat unloved and still covered in metal shavings. Of either Mikey or the gang, there was no sign.

Ru picked up a steel rod that was laying on one of the shelving units.

"Do you want one Steve?" she asked.

Steve shook his head.

"Not much use to me unless I can use it as a crutch".

With Ru leading the way and Steve sticking as close as he could behind whilst still giving himself every chance to scarper with his injuries if the need arisen, the pair slowly began to check for Mikey or indeed anyone else.

Ru felt her heart beating almost as if it were in her mouth. This was a bit too exciting even for her and it was only now that she truly realised that she had entered the lion's den. If there were anyone around, they could have knives, guns or anything. Hell, if there were enough of them, they wouldn't need any of that especially no-one knew they were here anyway.

After finding a few empty beer bottles, discarded pizza boxes and chip shop wrappers, Ru realised that if Mikey wasn't here now, then it's likely that someone had been here recently.

At the far end of the warehouse was a larger open space but before that were some old partitioned offices whose walls were partly removed and leaning over at a precarious and dangerous angle to one side. Above them was a mezzanine level accessed by a steel ladder staircase which led up to yet more metal shelving. Ru had the fright of her life when she casually looked in the gap between the stairs and the office wall to see a man with his back turned to her boiling a kettle.

Ru swore in her head and froze in her tracks. Thankfully she hadn't been noticed and ever so carefully, she walked backwards out of the line of sight of the shabbily dressed figure. Turning her head around, she put her finger to her lips to indicate to Steve he should stay silent before waving her arm about encouraging him to find a hiding spot in the shelving. Ru only just found time to run back herself when the man came out carrying three cups of tea, luckily he was too pre-occupied with his drinks to notice Ru clumsily hidden behind a box of rubber piping.

Once the man had disappeared to the far end of the warehouse, Ru sighed a deep breath of relief and tapped her pocket to make sure her asthma inhaler was still there.

"There's a guy who just made tea there" she whispered over to Steve.

"We should go and see if Mikey is there too?" Ru suggested.

Steve frowned, it seemed like a bad idea even though it was the entire point of coming here. It's just that he never imagined the crazy guy at the pub might have been talking some truth. What sort of people was Mikey hanging out with? Steve didn't know but he had a feeling that he would soon find out.

"Are you sure?" He asked with a tone in his voice that implied it would be best if Ru wasn't.

"I think there are three of them, going by how many cups that guy was holding. Listen you wait here and I'm going to climb up those stairs and see if I can see anything from up there." Ru said, explaining her plan.

Steve nodded his head in tacit acceptance and watched as Ru climbed the steel staircase as silently and stealthily as she could.

Ru looked all around when she got upstairs. It was quite a large area, perhaps the size of a tennis court. There was definitely no-one up there but as she crept on all fours to the far end, a number of things caught her attention now that she had a good view of the ground floor. Firstly there was an office chair sat right in the middle of the floor, it had some old rubber hosing tied around it which could possibly have been used as a rope. Above the chair was a large steel chain which was about 30 feet long and attached to an industrial crane that was somehow attached to the roof of the building.

Of more immediate concern were the voices that she could hear at the very end of the building. From her vantage point above Ru could see three people or, at least, their heads. They were sat on three more office chairs drinking as they gesticulated wildly with their arms. The whole area was covered in rubbish and food and more oil patches. Ru's eyes opened widely when she realised that the dark stains weren't oil but blood.

"Holy Shit!" she mouthed as the realisation came over her.

"These are some big-ass bad guys!"

As she couldn't see Mikey anywhere and was theoretically visible to one of the gang members, though he'd have to have almost X-ray eyes to see her, Ru she crouched down slowly and laid the steel rod down on the floor by her side.

Ru reached into her pocket and took out her phone and prayed that it was already on so it didn't make the start-up tone that would have alerted everyone that she was there.

"Let's take a photo of this lot" she smiled to herself at her genius though whether the photos would actually be useful in this low light was another matter.

She decided to stay and watch what was going on. By straining her ears, she could just about hear what was going on. In fact, the closest man was just about 10 feet away and if he farted she'd have a good idea what it was he had been eating last night.

"We need to find it," said one pony-tailed bruiser of a man.

"Do you know what it's worth", he continued.

"I know, I know," stammered an older man with grey hair "but he said he didn't have it".

Both men spoke in thick Russian accents and it made Ru wonder why they were speaking in English at all until the third in the group, a tall black guy started swearing at both of them. Do they have many black Russian gangsters? Ru wasn't sure but his voice sounded distinctly more Southend than St. Petersburg.

"He's never going to find it now is he? Not after you got The Wolves involved" blasted the older man at his black colleague.

Ru was entranced by it all and could have sat a good while longer until she noticed a spider on her hand. Ru hated spiders and though she had managed to avoid one of the girliest of screams that she frequently let out when finding a spider sharing the shower with her, she instinctively brushed the creature from her skin with her other hand. The spider was brushed away but her fingertips caught the steel rod and sent it rolling along the floor.

The group of men below sat in silence and for a moment Ru thought she might have got away with things.

"There is someone here?" said the old Russian.
"It's just the rats", the ponytail wearer suggested. "I've told him not to leave the pizza boxes everywhere," he said

as he motioned over to the black man who didn't take kindly to having to verbally defend himself while trying to enjoy his drink.

Ru stretched herself out as flat as she could on the floor and attempted to squirm away as the two Russian looked up roughly in her direction. Only when they were out of sight did she dare hurriedly raise herself into a crouching position.

"Go and check it out!" she heard one of the Russians bark.

Ru turned and ran for her life. Five seconds seemed like a lifetime as she rushed for the stairs, ran down the first four steps and then jumped about seven feet to the concrete floor below.

'Oh man!' she heard the voice in her head proclaim as she struggled to keep balance and not sprawl forward into a pile of boxes as the sound of footsteps behind her neared.

Ru turned to hurry Steve along but with a quick glance ahead, she saw he had already made a run for it, or a hobble anyway and was half way back to the hole they had broken in through.

"Oi, you stop!" her pursuer ordered.

Ru, however, wasn't going to stop for anything and caught up with Steve quite quickly just before they entered the shelved off area from which they had first come.

"Quickly, quickly," said Steve as Ru rushed past him and slid feet first through the loose metal walk sheet and back to the outside. Steve followed as fast he could but wasn't as fluid in motion as Ru was and he only just got out when an outstretched arm reached out towards his ankle.

Ru trod on the grasping arm as heavily as she could with her shoe and then kicked the aluminium sheeting with all her might just as a head was pushing its was clear. The man shouted his thanks in no uncertain terms as he was temporarily floored, allowing Ru and Steve to make their escape.

Ru could probably have scaled the fence in an emergency and this was an emergency but she couldn't leave Steve behind and so helped him run as fast as he could back to the gap in the fence. By the time the black gang member was nearing them, they were safely on the other side of the fence.

Though they couldn't see him for bushes and parked vehicles, Ru could tell the man was persistent and that they wouldn't easily make it back to their car. Just around the corner and a little way down the road were the three industrial waste bins that they had passed before they entered the warehouse. Ru opened the first of them but it was full of black bin bags and so she let the lid drop loudly before opening the second container. There were still lots of rubbish inside but, at least, there was room to climb in.

Somehow Steve managed to get his legs inside and Ru pulled down the lid just before their pursuer rounded the corner but he was in agony and even though he tried his best to conceal his whimpering. If Ru could hear it then so could anyone else so she clamped her hand over his mouth for a few seconds until he had calmed down. It was pitch black inside and they did their best to bury themselves beneath the upper layers of rubbish. It was damp and it stank to high heaven but hopefully, it was safe and gave them a chance to catch their breath.

A few minutes later a pair of footsteps could be heard jogging over to them. They footsteps stopped outside the bins and Ru froze in terror. She could feel the hairs rise on the back of her neck as the man lifted up the lid of the first container. He rummaged around inside a little and then slammed the lid shut.

Both Ru and Steve expected it to be their turn next and their hearts were in their mouths but they were unexpectedly granted a little bit of relief when the man walked past them to the third bin. He lifted the lid up, muttered a few words of industrial language and let the thick plastic lid drop down with a bang.

"We're next" Ru whispered to Steve as she prepared herself for a fight.

All set to jump out, they heard the man walk back to their second bin. He put his hand on the handle of the lid and stopped, took a deep breath and punched the bin, shocking Ru as the amplified noise reverberated around inside. What the man did not do however was lift up the lid and instead, he dejectedly trotted back towards the den in the abandoned warehouse.

Ru and Steve waited a good minute before they let out a sigh of relief and another thirty before they dared move. When at last Ru decided to check that the coast was clear, she got herself tangled up in some bin bags and inadvertently sent Steve face first into the rubbish.

"Oh shit! Oh no," he moaned.

"I'm sorry Steve, I got stuck... just a second".

"I think I'm bleeding again".

Ru found her footing and gingerly pushed the lid of the bin up just enough to see that there was no-one nearby. In fact, she was quite relieved to find that their pursuer wasn't standing right next to the bin. With her eyes darting back and forth, it became apparent that the street was again empty allowing her to push the bin lid over. She was just clambering out when Steve let out a scream of horror that she would remember for the rest of her life.

Looking round she just about saw Steve lying on top of a bloodied and beaten body before a split second later Steve instinctively leapt three feet across to the other side of the bin before furiously trying to jump out.

The shock of what she saw coupled with Steve's understandable recoil made Ru scream out loud too and that in turn panicked Steve, who lost his grip and fell back onto the body before jumping instantly back up and taking Ru's outstretched hand. Ignoring all his pain, Steved was half pulled out and half climbed out but it was in such a blind panic that the momentum was too much for Ru to handle and he toppled her over backwards and a second later they were both sprawled in a tangle on the black tarmac road.

Steve rolled over and started wiping his blood covered hands on his trousers and then even on the tarmac of the road, not noticing that blood was also all smeared over his face. Ru left Steve to compose himself and walked up to the bin and peered inside. The blood that was on Steve, however, wasn't Steve's blood and there was a very dead body inside the bin. Covered in cuts and bruises was a battered body. Ru let out a torturous yelp and closed her eyes, not just at the sight that met her eyes but the unexpected wave of emotion that washed over her. She'd come here to find her friend and now she had. The body inside was that of Mikey.

Chapter 5

"This one's taken", Ru spoke out as someone tried to get into her toilet cubicle.

The person got a similar response in the next toilet cubicle before finally finding a vacant cubicle. The toilet block returned to its silent calm which Ru really, really appreciated.

Work had been incredibly busy all day and Ru felt it was the last place she wanted to be. The only place that she could find a little respite was here, the staff toilets in the supermarket.

She still couldn't quite believe it. Mikey was dead. Mikey! She'd only seen him a few days earlier. What on earth had happened to him? What on earth had she and Steve got into the middle of? Whoever they were, they meant business and weren't just messing around. Seriously, if they killed Mikey and beat up Steve, anything could happen to her or Steve and that unease and fear tempered slightly the utter shock of seeing Mikey laying bloodied and beaten in the industrial waste bin.

When they had got home last night, the atmosphere veered between total silence and near hysteria. Steve couldn't get over the horror of the moment when he had been laying on his dead friend and no matter how much he washed himself, the imaginary blood he was soaked in was much harder to remove than the actual blood of Mikey.

Ru thanked her lucky stars that neither she or Steve had got injured and thanks to their balaclavas it is unlikely that they were identified. In fact, Ru thought that they may not even have realised that there were two people involved as it was likely their pursuer only saw Ru herself.

Steve and Ru had debated all evening as to what to do and as neither could sleep they had talked deep into the night too. Should they call the police? Mikey had been murdered, their flat broke into and Steve beaten to a pulp. Steve had advocated contacting the police but for some reason, Ru wasn't keen on it. Whether it was because she feared the gang coming back? That wasn't really what stopped her though she did worry whether the police would be able to protect them at all.

As it turned out, it was a moot point. Sitting around on his own at home, the tension and horror had obviously got the better of Steve and he had phoned up Sgt Wilkinson a few hours earlier. The Sergeant took Steve down to the warehouse but there was no-one there and more to the point there was absolutely no sign of Mikey in any of the waste bins out on the street. Steve felt a right plonker but there was something in his statement that made the Sergeant consider it to be a lead of some sort.

Apparently Steve had given the Sgt some of his bloodied clothing to see if the police could cross-check it against DNA samples from Mikey's flat but from the text messages Ru had received, Steve wasn't convinced he was being believed by the officer but surely the tests would speak for themselves sooner or later.

Ru didn't blame Steve for contacting the police, she was torn over doing so herself. She did though feel shocked at finding Mikey dead like that amongst all the rubbish and she had spent much of the morning wondering what it was that Mikey had got involved in that was so important... so wrong. Why couldn't he tell anyone? Apparently, it must have happened quickly as there were no real signs that anything so wrong was in the air when she last talked to him at breakfast on his birthday.

Ru flushed the toilet. She hadn't come into the cubicle to use the toilet but having spent so long inside and with the neighbouring booths occupied she felt the need to play up to the role. She washed her hands and face and made her way back to the pharmacy. It was 2 pm and she still had several hours left on her shift.

"I can't do this today" she sighed to herself as she reached the counter. Her manager overheard her.

"Is everything ok Ru", Nadine asked while not even looking up from the prescription she was measuring out.

Ru shook her head.

"Something happened yesterday and I need to go home. I don't suppose I can leave early can I?" Ru spoke with a slight quiver hoping against hope that her boss would look upon the request with some sympathy.

"Mary will be in at 4 pm anyway," said Ru trying to, at least, convince herself that it wouldn't upset too many things at work.

"Wait till Suzie or Julie gets back from their lunch and then you can go".

Wow! Ru hadn't expected that. It was almost unheard of for anyone to be allowed to go home like this unless they were looking and feeling like a zombie.   It put a little spring in her step for a few seconds and was enough to convince her that she could make it another 15 minutes without collapsing in a tearful heap in the consultation room.

Ru took the time to reconcile some prescription receipts until Suzie came back from lunch and then with a brief apology, made her excuses and left the store. Thank heavens Nige the security guard wasn't in today otherwise by 3 pm the whole of the supermarket would know something was up and knowing Nige it would probably involve drink or pregnancy.

There was little traffic on the way home so Ru decided to make a detour to the gym where she took out her frustration on the treadmill and cross-body trainer until even that wasn't taking her mind off things and so she made her way home.

As Ru climbed the stairs up to their flat, she experienced a funny sensation. It was a good job Ru was teetotal. Otherwise, she could have swore that she needed a drink.

"You're home early Rhubarb, is everything ok"? Steve asked.

Ru walked over to the kitchen and dropped her bag and keys loudly on the worktop before pouring herself a glass of soya milk from the fridge.

"I couldn't concentrate, how could anyone?" Ru replied vacantly.

"I know... I hope you're ok with me calling the police? Steve asked.

"Of course, I am, how could I not be? We can't worry about ourselves too much. Someone killed Mikey and they have to pay one way or the other," Ru opined.

"Listen, I have an idea. Why don't we order some pizzas and watch a BluRay? They do gluten free ones now and we can grate some goats cheese on one for you," Ru suggested.

Being gluten and dairy intolerant were just two things that Ru and Steve had in common. Ru had it worse of course as she was a Vegan too and not as everyone assumed because of her religion.... everyone thinks that when she tells them as if people with brown skin can't be kind to animals like everyone else.

"Deal sis, I'll order some on the website," said Steve, newly invigorated.

"So what did the police say to you?" Ru asked.

"Not much, I'm not sure they believed me. They took my top which had all the blood on it but I felt a right idiot when we went there and Mikey wasn't there," Steve answered, shrugging his shoulders.

As Ru thought through the events of the day before for the thousandth time in her head, she remembered that she had got some photos of the gang in the warehouse yesterday.

"I forgot about these Steve," she said.

Ru delved into her bag and pulled out her phone.

"I took these of the three guys who were in the warehouse yesterday. I know they're not great quality but do you recognise them from when they came to the flat?"

Ru handed Steve the phone who quickly glanced at it before swearing under his breath.

"He's big!" Steve was shocked at the size of the man in the photo.

Ru peered over his shoulder. She must have pressed a button when she handed Steve the phone as the photo wasn't of any of the gang.

"Oh, not Roman", she shrieked

Ru was slightly flustered that Steve had seen she the WWE wrestler on her phone.

"Sorry!"

She gave Steve the phone back and he studied it a bit more intently.

"It's a bit hard to make out isn't it? I don't think it is them, though, I mean one of those guys hasn't just got a ponytail but a full blown mane and none of the ones that did this to me were like that".

"That's strange. Anyway, how are you wounds today?" Ru asked.

"Getting better I guess, from a low starting point, though. I just need to rest and if it wasn't hard enough to get sleep before, after yesterday It is nearly impossible

"Why don't you use those pills you got prescribed?" Ru asked.

"I don't like taking tablets."

"Better than suffering and some rest might help you feel better", Ru said.

Ru hoped that with her being a pharmacist that her opinion might actually count for something and she saw Steve thinking it over as he handed Ru her phone back.

"Either it's a big ass gang or more than one group are involved in this big mess", he continued as he lowered himself slowly onto the sofa before finally collapsing somewhat in a heap.

"How about we get an Indian tonight?" he said.

"What, you're not happy with just me?" Ru giggled.

"Sure why not. You sort out the order and I'll go and shower. Maybe we can watch a movie on demand too?"

"Nice one Ru", Steve shouted across the room as he watched Ru disappear into the bathroom.

*   *   *

It was about 9.30pm, or so it was the last time Steve checked his iPad which always seemed to be welded to his lap in the evenings like some comforting toy that a toddler might carry around with him. Between the two of them, they had finished off some Bombay aloo, spicy rice and curries. As usual, Steve had gone for the Chicken Balti while Ru had gone for the tried and trusted veggie Jalfrezi. Ru had made some gluten free naan bread in the oven which they used to soak up the sauces. Now all that was left was a few Poppadoms and an ever decreasing amount of mango chutney that needed to be mopped up. The lights were off and the pair were doing their best to have a relaxed evening.

On the TV screen, Gerard Butler was busy mopping up some North Koreans in the latter stages of Olympus Has Fallen. The surround sound was on louder than normal as there was no Mikey across the way and the flat below seemed to be inhabited by semi-deaf pensioners who obviously didn't seem to hear either Mikey's place or Ru's getting smashed to smithereens in recent days.

The air echoed to shooting, swearing and quite a bit of belching though most of the latter was coming from the sofa rather than the TV. Being quite a fan of the Scottish hunk, Ru felt if the movie ran out of money and Gerard was going to belch everyone to death then it would still be worth watching.

As stupid as it later seemed to both Ru and Steve, at the time, they didn't quite appreciate how real life was mimicking what was happening on screen. Suddenly their main living room window smashed open. Glass went flying everywhere and there was barely time to swear when three men pushed through the broken shards and blowing curtains.

For a split second neither Ru or Steve moved as they were seemingly frozen on the sofa before Ru sprang into action. Ru ran towards the kitchenette and grabbed the biggest carving knife that was to hand but by the time she had turned round the three men had already surrounded Steve and one of them had his hand firmly around Steve's neck.

"Put it down before I put him down" growled the aggressor as he motioned that he would throw Steve out of the window.

Ru momentarily weighed up the options and slowly reached down and placed the knife on the floor.

"Smart and hot, I like it," the intruder commented before releasing Steve from the stranglehold.

"Who are you… what do you want, why are you here?" Ru asked.

"We're the Wolves, we're looking for something which we've been told is here."

Steve didn't recognise any of the three as being amongst those who broke in an smashed up the place and incidentally himself a few days earlier

"I'm Wakim," said the big burly man who was looking down at Steve.

"We've been sent to find something very important".

Steve stood up slowly having only now recovered his breath.

"I've already told that Ivo guy that we don't have any money and we don't know where Mikey kept his, not that he ever had any… he always seemed to owe money not store it."

"Ivo has been here?" asked a slender darkly dressed Asian man, no older than in his mid-twenties.

"Who the hell are you?   I thought Jihadi John was dead?" Steve quipped.

The Arab muttered something which Ru couldn't make out but it seemed likely he wanted to smash Steve's face in even more but was stopped by Wakim who physically intervened.

"Well, what is it you're looking for?" Ru asked.

"Drugs", Wakim replied.

"I'm a pharmacist, might I refer you to your local supermarket… better hurry though they close at 10 pm," Ru replied.

With that, a third man who had thus far remained silent grabbed a vase and threw it a Ru who ducked just in time and it soared past her face, eventually smashing into the side of the fridge freezer.

"This is a particular drug. You seen anything here?", Wakim.

"Listen, if this is about Mikey, he didn't live here, he was in the flat opposite. Why don't you have a mosey around there?" Ru didn't just ask but by the tone of her voice, demanded.

"We already did, we didn't find anything and besides that place has been turned upside down".

"That would be Ivo. He didn't find anything either", Steve chipped in.

"Look Mikey's dead, you better leave. I'm sick of my place getting fucked up!" Ru seethed.

Their attention momentarily on Ru, Steve kneed Wakim in the groin. He made a good connection and the man was soon doubled over. Ru saw her moment to strike, she took two steps forward and jumped through the air kicking one of the intruders on his face and sending him straight through the broken window. He didn't even have the chance to clutch at the curtains before falling with a scream into the garden below.

The third man looked on in astonishment and took a wild swing at Ru but only succeeded in striking thin air. With cat like reflexed Ru sprung up and dealt him a perfect 1-2 punch combination which sent him sprawled woozily to the laminate floor but somehow managed to pull himself up by the curtains. Ru was all ready to deck him more permanently but the curtains came loose in his hand and he fell back through the shattered glass and into the black night beyond.

Both Steve and Ru laughed as it was such a comical sight.

"Are you ok?" Steve asked?

Ru nodded. "And you?"

"Let's get them!" Ru said.

"Really, that's crazy!" Steve said who nevertheless made every effort to keep up with Ru as she headed for the door. It was clearly a hopeless case though and Ru was already outside side before Steve was halfway down the stairs.

He went outside clutching his ribs to see Ru scouring the undergrowth beneath the windows. It was hard to see in the dark but it was clear that all three had somehow left the scene.

"Wow, they're tough Mofo's," Ru said.

"Or you scared the shit out of them more like" Steve countered.

Suddenly, Steve caught some movement about 100 yards down the street from the communal car park.

"They heading down the alley to the back of the estate!" he shouted.

"I'll get them," Ru said.

Steve put his hand on Ru to stop her.

"No, its dangerous and dark and I can't keep up". Steve pleaded.

"Look I can go on my bike and flush them out, you can drive round and cut them off at the pass!"

Ru gave Steve her 'Are you crazy look', or at least, she meant to but it was too dark for it to be seen.

"You can't even run let alone ride", she yelled.

"My legs are fine, it's everything else that's knackered". The pair went back into the block of flats, Steve grabbed his bike from under the stairs whilst Ru ran back to the apartment and grabbed her car keys. When she fired up her car, to her surprise Steve had already gone vanished into the night.

Steve was breathing heavily and going as fast as he could. There were occasional street lights but the alley was dark with several places to hide. For some reason though he didn't feel as scared as he thought he might. Perhaps some of Ru's combativeness has rubbed off on him but he thought the gang to clearly on the run and desperate to escape rather than wanting to stand and fight.

He stopped at the first two turn-offs and shouted out loudly. There was no-one there and, to be honest, he didn't want to meet anyone, he wanted to make his presence so well known that the gang had ample time to flee and hopefully they would escape right into Ru. He had no idea that Ru was so awesome. Wow!

"I'm gonna kill you," Steve shouted as he carried on riding until at last he thought he caught sight of the three walking under a lamppost about 100 feet away.

Steve swore to himself in his head as he chased them down the alley, happily they didn't seem to be aware that he was in no shape to fight anyone and when he shouted again they ran off. His sides were aching but no more than when he hobbled from the sofa to the toilet.

In a matter of seconds he had reached the brightly lit lamp and a few deep breaths later he was out of the alley and back on to the streets. He was gaining on them but not as quickly as he dreaded, maybe he was sorer than he imagined.   They were heading towards a block of garages which Steve knew led to open woodland.

Soon he became aware of a car engine and headlights coming up behind him, he thought he was going to get knocked over when it slowed down. The window was already down and he was relieved to see it was his flatmate.

"Wow Steve, you can move on that thing, where are they?" Ru asked.

Steve might have been able to move but he wasn't really able to breathe as he was rather out of breath.

"They're up ahead… three of them heading for the garages", he panted.

Ru nodded

"See you later Stevey boy!" she said as she put her foot down and despite his best efforts, Ru soon left him eating dust as she roared off with a smile on her face.

Seconds later she was onto them but they, in turn, were just about onto the garages. She drove right at them and locked in a handbrake turn. Her car swung round and clipped one of the gang and sent him to the ground. He was unhurt though and was soon back with his mates giving a leg up to Wakim onto the roof of the garage.

Ru jumped out of the car and launched herself at the two still on the ground. Her adrenaline and enthusiasm gave her extra strength and she took down both the men.

"You crazy bitch," said Wakim just before Ru rammed his face into her knee.

The third man pulled at the guttering to get up onto the roofs of the garage but only succeeded in pulling it down. Turning disappointment to his advantage, he swung round and brought it down over Ru's back which sent her sprawling as the drain pipe fell apart about her.

She was not badly hurt but was unable to stop the other two gang members from finally hoisting themselves onto the roof of the garage. Still she gave it her best shot and grabbed on to the final dangling leg and rammed it into the wall before he got away.

Wakim peered over the edge of the roof and looked down on Ru, spitting at her. The globule landed on her leg but it didn't bother her much.

"Who the hell are you?" he demanded.

Ru paused for a moment, took a deep breath and replied.

"I'm Vixen!"

Just then Steve arrived on his bike and Wakim and the gang disappeared into the night.

Chapter 6

To the surprise of both Ru and Steve, the police were
extremely quick in reacting to their call. It seemed that
they had finally surpassed the threshold needed for things
to be taken seriously. Minutes later the police arrived and
asked their usual questions and took away a few things for
their investigations.

Sgt. Wilkinson was back and when Ru and Steve ran
through things with him, he immediately offered them a
safe house due to concerns that their lives were in danger.
Ru and Steve both agreed in an instant but the wind was
rather blown out of their sails when they were told it
would have to wait until tomorrow as it was too late now
to do anything.

Upon seeing their reaction, Sgt. Wilkinson offered to have a
protection officer stay under their window until the
morning. Ru voiced that it would be a good idea whilst
Steve couldn't have nodded any more profusely than what
he did.

The flat once more tidied up and the broken window now
boarded up, the pair went to bed for a restless nights sleep.
Ru was thankful that she had the next day off from work.
She hated the situation that they were in but she felt such a
thrill when things all kicked off. She loved the buzz and
wanted to experience more of it but she felt awful about
Mikey and Steve. Even though Mikey's death had nothing
to do with Ru, she somehow felt responsible for it and
definitely for what happened to Steve. How could all of

this happen? Mikey was happy and ready for his birthday just a few days ago. Steve wouldn't hurt a fly and now look at him. She knew the police were well-meaning but…

It was almost Ru she felt a responsibility to sort things out but it was a heavy responsibility. She knew she might do something but could she? Should she? Ru put on her favourite track by 30 STM and lit some candles on her dressing table. Though she was gazing into the mirror, she was, in fact, looking deep into her soul.

Knowing the song off by heart she began singing along, the words reaching into her heart, her eyes beginning to well up with tears.

" what if I wanted to fight, beg for the rest of my life, what would you do? You say you wanted more, what are you waiting for, I'm not running from you.. Come break me down, bury me bury me .. I am finished with you."

She put the track on repeat play and crawled into bed, the familiarity of the music and dancing flames of the candle eventually lulling her to a restless though short-lived sleep.

Ru woke with a start, something in the lyrics of the music that was still playing even now, had caused her to have an early morning brainwave, or at least that is how she thought of it. What if she were to be a little pro-active in getting justice for Mikey? Maybe she could have a little bit of fun at the same time as putting to use some her combat skills that she outside of competition, she never got to use. Something like Batman would do, allowing her to keep her day-job and then at night stalk the street taking on the scum and villainy of the world. Maybe she could get a costume made up! No that would be taking a bit too far... or would it?

"Hmmm", she would give that some thought.

Obviously, she would have to have some sort of persona rather than being plain old Ru Barard. She needed a name, an identity. As an actor or wrestler wearing a mask, it would allow her to get into character and play up to the part she was going to write for herself. Damn, Catwoman for taking the most obvious name. Maybe Amazon she thought? No, besides she was an Apple girl.

"Yes!" she shouted as punched the air with near delight. She wasn't sure where she got the idea of her Vixen alter-ego, it came to her on the spur of the moment but she liked it. It conveyed a sense of a beautiful cat, nice to look at but agile, strong and feisty with claws that could quickly turn into weapons that could beat most men.

It wasn't their fault, most guys were helpless to resist a beautiful woman in any case and Ru thought that it could be an important weapon in her arsenal. What could be more dangerous than a gorgeous woman who ensnares her victims, with a brain to outthink them and then by the time they may just begin to suspect something is amiss, she had the physical prowess to knock them out.

Most importantly of all though Ru thought was that she had the motivation and she always got what she wanted even if it was through discipline and hard work, those long hours at the gym were a testament to that. Her friend had been murdered, their home violated twice in a week and Steve hospitalised and then almost killed again last night. It was time someone stood up to these people but it wouldn't be Ru, it would be Vixen. Or maybe just V in the heat of battle.

Unable to sleep and full of ideas, she leapt out of bed and put her dressing gown on before tiptoeing out to the living room. Thankfully Steve was in bed so she powered up his iMac. This was going to be too cool!

As the computer powered up, she went to her handbag looking for some lipstick. There was plenty to choose from but which would be most suitable. Black? No, too goth for a superhero. Brown? Maybe but that was more for work as it went well with her uniform and she could hardly be a vigilante dressed in white overalls. No, that would never work besides Spiderman already had that covered with his whole laboratory outfit thing.

"Yes!"

She had found what she was looking for and switching on the camera on the iMac to use it as a mirror, she proceeded to apply her lipstick. It lay somewhere between blood red and burgundy in the colour table. It screamed seductive and dangerous.

"Very V", Ru assured herself.

Then she got a white serviette from the kitchen and pressed it gently but firmly upon her lips before pulling it away again. As she had hoped the lipstick had come off on the serviette leaving a perfectly alluring kiss mark upon it.

Next up she switched on the scanner, it made a loud noise as it powered up and Ru checked to see if Steve's bedroom was still dark and was relieved to find that it was. There was no need for Steve to know about all this, at least not yet.

Having put the serviette down on the scanner surface, she made a high-resolution scan before opening up paint brush. The scan had come up well and after a few minutes of tinkering, she had completed the design. Next up she had to find the cards, she knew Steve had a box of them in one of the drawers under his iMac as he used them a lot for his freelance work by printing his own he found it easier to tailor his card to his new or potential clients.

Finding them underneath some papers and envelopes, Ru thought to herself that ideally she didn't want to be traced by her cards and so went back into her room and returning, wearing a pair of gloves, she put a sheet of cards into the printer.

"Let's be optimistic," she said to herself as she loaded in the second sheet of cards and took her gloves off again to operate the computer.

She stopped for a moment to check everything was all set up and tapped her nails on the desk before clicking the mouse on 'print'. A few seconds later and before her eyes, a succession of printed cards came out of the printer. These weren't going to be business cards, though; no these were going to be calling cards and part of the mystery and identity of Vixen.

With a gloved hand, she picked the first card up and brought it up close to her face so as to admire it. The card looked great. On a plain shiny white card was her dark lipstick kiss with a large red V in a handwriting-like font followed by a small 'x' kiss.

She put the cards away, emailed the files back to her own address and deleted all evidence that she had ever been on the machine. It was 6 am and time to go to the gym, she always liked it there the most when it was early in the morning as there was barely anyone around and she could put in some effort without getting distracted or having an audience.

By the time she returned, Steve was up and beginning the process of packing stuff away ready to move. By packing, it wasn't much more than piling most belongings into bin bags and cardboard boxes. Only the electrical items were given a special service with more care and effort into ensuring they would survive the move. Neither Ru or Steve knew how long they would be gone from their flat, the broken window was being replaced but that only made things look normal on the outside. The truth was that they both felt unsafe even if neither explicitly said so if only because they didn't want to worry the other.

Their new place was only five miles away and was actually in a nice quiet location. Ru thought it was almost too nice a place, she'd never normally be able to afford it on her salary. It was a small 2 bedroom semi-detached house in a new development, it even had its own driveway and satellite TV for free. Ru thought it was rather like arriving at a holiday cottage as at first it felt comfortable but in an impersonal sort of way but three or four hours spent filling it with their belongings following four return car trips to their old place and it was soon beginning to feel bit more like home.

By late afternoon, Ru was beginning to think about her first night out as V. She planned to tell Steve that she was going out with work friends for a drink, that would give her the chance to dress up nicely without arousing too many suspicions. She had planned to wear some high heel boots that added several inches to her already 5'6" inch frame coupled with some black leather trousers and a matching jacket. Oh yes with a certain burgundy lipstick to match.

She didn't have much info to go on but remembered what Danny said a week or more back about how the gang that held Mikey often went to Diamonds. She didn't know the big picture of how everything fixed together but she was determined to find out and get some justice at the same time. When she felt suitably dressed up, she stepped out of her room and immediately caught Steve's attention.

"Shit Ru, you're looking smoking hot tonight!", Steve said for once looking up from his iMac.

"Do you want me to drive you?" he asked.

"No, I'm good thanks. You just rest up and try and relax a bit".

Steve came over to give Ru a hug.

"Be careful, don't talk to any strange men… well except that security guy".

"What's that for?" said Ru, not quite expecting a hug.

"I worry about you… I don't want you to get hurt", Steve confessed.

"If you don't want me to go, I don't have to, I understand". Ru asked before continuing "Don't worry, it's just drinks and I don't even drink…"

Ru reached down and grabbed Steve's hand.

"Besides, I'm a good 2 inches taller than you. I'll be just fine".

Steve nodded his head with a wry smile before Ru grabbed her car keys

Ru was glad that they weren't in the block of flats, it was nice not to have to walk down the communal stairs especially in boots like these. She was excited about the night to come and only felt bad about having to tell Steve a white lie which felt all the worse when he waved goodbye to her through the window as she reversed out of the drive.

She had been to Diamonds before with friends, it was a fun place and they usually had some great live music. She wasn't really aware though that dodgy people hung out there, well not any more than in most clubs of the size.

Luckily the hotel above the club had a car park so Ru was able to drive almost up to the front door.

Ru quickly checked her mirror to make sure that she was still looking good, grabbed her bag and walked right past the stares of the two security guys on the door who followed her in with their eyes until she was out of sight.

The club was busy but it wasn't heaving, Ru thought perhaps that was because it was a Thursday night. Diamonds was split into four distinct areas, with two halls with dance and trance music and though Ru liked a dance as much as any girl and the lights did look seriously awesome, she was here on business. In the centre was a bar area which she stopped at to get a lemonade. Whilst she waited to get served, her attention was drawn to the stage on the left where there was a lively song being sung by a live band which was playing a tune which tugged at her rock chick roots.

Ru sat herself down at an angle where she could watch the band but also keep an eye out for anyone from the gang. She knew it was a bit of a long-shot as they may not come here at all let alone tonight but she guessed that none of the gang were the types who would like dance music and that they most likely came here to pick up women.

The band was good, the lead singer Stefano Giorgini was giving it his all and Ru thought he looked quite cute as he strutted his stuff, she wasn't the only one going by the reaction he was getting from the crowd.

Ru thought Stefano to be a not too bad looking Italian albeit with a strong American accent no doubt due to his time spent most time gigging in Los Angeles. He was a slim build, around 5"7' tall. Good looking, dark hair that tended to fall into a curl to one side and shaved around the back. He wore a loose t-shirt imprinted with a few logos which Ru couldn't make out in the light, skin tight grey jeans and black ankle boots whilst holding onto the smooth white bass guitar. Ru decided to look them up on Google and found their videos on Youtube. To her surprise, she saw he was using the same guitar here as on his Text Message video she was watching online.

The coloured light fell perfectly on the band on stage with a very chilled atmosphere and in the corner stood an old sound guy leaning against his controls ensuring the amps and bass were performing in line. Ru really liked it. She also liked the guitarist too, she'd always had a thing for bald guys ever since Captain Picard.

I don't know where I'm at this point
Can't find my way
Through pieces of my life…
I'm gonna get around them
Angels around me got my back
What can I do?

Ru would have happily listened to Stefano all night long but her attention was grabbed by the appearance at the bar of precisely the three men that she had seen in that old warehouse that she and Steve had sneaked into a few days ago. She was sure it was them, especially as no-one else would sport a ponytail like the younger Russian. In fact, she thought that the older guy was even wearing the same clothes as in the warehouse.

Ru watched the trio order some drinks, at least, the black man had dressed up a bit. She knew she didn't have a chance against all three at once and besides she was here to get information as much as anything else. After a few minutes, two tall blonde girls walked up to the bar and were immediately accosted by the two Russians. She couldn't quite see what was going on but a few minutes later the girls paired off with the Russians and led them back to a large table leaving the young black guy looking somewhat lonely up at the bar. It was now or never.

Ru took a large sip of lemonade and strutted over to the bar a few feet left of the lonesome gang member. Before the Ru even got the attention of the barmaid, she felt a nudge on her arm.

"I can get this if you like... what you having?"

Ru turned round and smiled as if she had just set eyes on the man of her dreams. It was the young gangster.

"Oh thank-you, that's so sweet... a Pimms please".

"Excuse me, a pint of lager for me and a Pimms for this lovely lady please".

"My name's Paul by the way", the young man flustered.

"V, my name is V". Ru said trying to sound convincing.

"That's a cute name for a girl", remarked Paul.

"That's a cute smile for a guy" she smiled back.

Paul motioned for them to go back and sit with his two friends but Ru convinced him to come to her quiet corner so she could listen to the music too.

They sat down and it quickly became obvious that Paul fancied the pants of Ru. Unfortunately for him, even if the circumstances were different, he wasn't her type and too young too. Still she thought that he needn't let him know that.

"I've not seen you here before?" Paul asked.

"I haven't been here for years. I'm on business tonight," Ru replied.

"Really?" said Paul seemingly a bit shocked.

"No, stupid. Not that sort of business" said Ru as she put her hand on his thigh.

"I'm a chemist, just meeting some friends" explained Ru.

"What about you?" she asked him as she reached into her handbag with her spare hand.

"Your friends aren't pigs are they"? Paul asked.

Ru took a small tissue out of her bag and put it on the table next to her drink before taking a sip. She let out a nervous laugh.

"No, mostly shop workers though one or two can be hard work. Why do you ask?"

Paul drew closer to Ru to try and ensure his voice wouldn't carry which was unlikely anyway given the loud music.

"I'm in a gang!" he announced.

Ru tried to appear impressed.

"No way, really? I should have guessed, that's probably why you're so confident and sexy" she nodded her head in affirmation.

Paul laughed and took several nervous gulps from his pint of lager.

"I've got two mates here too if you'd like to meet them", he explained.

Ru smiled as a voice in her head said in no uncertain terms that that was not going to happen.

"Not yet though as I want to get to know you," Ru said as seductively as she could.

Ru ran her hand up Paul's body and gave him a peck on the lips and with his attention easily distracted, emptied the contents of her tissue into his drink with her spare hand before giving it a quick swirl to ensure the mixture had all dissolved.

Ru's move had Paul totally fall for her and she almost felt a bit sorry for him as he was not only out of his depth but she was out of his league.

"Tell me a bit about your gang" Ru purred.

"It's not my gang, I'm the dogsbody of it but I'm going to progress. We're The Bears", Paul said before taking a drink.

"Wow, that is so cool", Ru said doing her best to look smitten as Paul lost himself in her big brown eyes.

On the outside Ru might be looking like the hottest girl in the club but inside she had butterflies as she worried whether Paul would notice that she had tampered with his drink.

"We normally sell drugs but things have got a bit out of hand recently and someone ended up dead".

"You didn't kill him did you"? Ru asked.

Paul took another swig of lager and shook his head.

"I don't think so, that's the funny thing, no-one seems to know. It's weird".

Ru watched Paul intently. Before she had left home, she had taken three of Steve's sleeping pills out of their soluble shells and put the powder in the tissue. She didn't know how long it would take to work but she didn't think it would be too long given that the normal dosage was only two pills and with the outer shell removed, the drugs would be absorbed even quicker into his blood stream especially with the alcohol.

Even now she noticed that Paul's eyes were beginning to stare vacantly ahead if he didn't realise he was getting tired, he soon would Ru thought.

"Whose in charge of the gang, is it one of those two guys at the bar?"

Paul let out a long sigh and his speech became slower and a little bit of an effort, or so Ru thought.

"No, that's Drew. He never comes here, he barely leaves his hotel suite? I've never even met him".

Paul frowned somewhat, was it because he saw Ru roll her eyes a little at his reply or did he suspect something was wrong? Ru wasn't sure which and, to be honest, she hadn't thought any further ahead.

"I should get back to Vladimir and Sergei".

Paul made to get up. He swayed a little as if he had had a lot more than the three-quarters of a pint of lager which he had drank.

"No! You can't go!"

Ru was startled that he even thought of leaving her. This could ruin everything before things even got started and the tone of her voice alarmed Paul forcing Ru to act quickly.

"I mean stay and finish your drink with me first, I don't get to drink with hot guys like you every day" before promptly tugging on his arm and pulling him back down. Ru hadn't done this before and wasn't sure whether he had to drink more before he fell asleep or whether he had already had enough and it just needed more time. The only thing she knew was that having him going to the others would have them onto her in a flash and things wouldn't be much better if he collapsed dramatically on the tables half way there.

Ru sat on his lap and smiled as she saw him becoming confused before her eyes. She reached over and took a sip of her Pimms before encouraging Paul to drink up the end of his. He lifted his glass up to his mouth before putting it back on the table and so Ru lifted it up to him and literally poured it slowly into his mouth and didn't move the glass until he swallowed it.

She felt the strength begin to seep from his body and his hand that had hitherto been pushing quite firmly to get her off his lap sagged onto her leg.

"Listen, I'm a cop. I'm not going to bust you if you can tell me who else is involved in all this... The Walkers?"

Paul's eyes widened at the mention of cops and for a while it brought a bit of energy back into him and Ru had to lean all her weight on him to keep him back against the green leather sofa.

"Yes The Walkers, maybe The Wolves too".

"Good boy!"

"Why do we have to talk about this, how about we go to my car?", he said as he tried to kiss Ru which made her giggle.

"I don't think you're up to it at the moment. You're just a boy really", Ru teased.

Paul spoke quietly, his eyes repeatedly shutting and reopening focusing intently on Ru but even if he knew nothing about it, Ru knew he only had a few moments left.

"I think you should get out of this business Paul, I'm going to sort out your friends… you're not going to have a gang by the time I get through with things".

Paul shook his head and in his head shouted out 'no', in reality, though it was little more than a whisper. Ru lay more heavily on Paul and he sank into the leather, his head laying backwards. For about a minute she sat on him this way, he twice feebly tried to lift his head up but each time took more of an effort. He closed his eyes once, opened them briefly again and then fell asleep.

She looked around and saw that no-one had even noticed what had happened. She quickly checked inside Paul's wallet but there was no useful information at all and unusually he didn't seem to have a phone with him.

She clambered off Paul whose head was now slowly drooping onto his chest and took a sip of Pimms before retrieving a glove from her bag, she very excitedly took out her very first calling card and put it in Paul's hand.   Ru looked down on her helpless victim with a broad grin and decided to take a photo for posterity. Vixen had lured her first victim to his doom and what's more, she had got some extremely valuable information.

Chapter 7

"One down, two to go", Ru said to herself as she picked up her drink and went back to the bar. The bar was a bit more crowded now so rather than wait to be served for a new drink she decided to head to the toilets to freshen up.

She took a slightly longwinded route through the tables in the general direction of the toilets and walked as slowly, slinkily and close to Vladimir and Sergei as she dared to. Getting their attention was one thing but raising their suspicions was something else entirely. As she walked past she looked over her shoulder and cast a smile in the direction of Sergei. He saw it and it instantly got his attention and that of the lady he was with. It immediately caused the woman who he was drinking with to raise her voice at him when she noticed he was staring at Ru.

By the time Ru entered the ladies, ignoring protests and threats from his companion, Sergei was making his excuses at the table and Ru was sure that he would accidentally on purpose bump into her in the very near future.

The ladies toilets were empty except for a teenage girl who was washing her face after apparently vomiting in the toilets. 'Classy' Ru thought to herself as she watched the girl walk out as Ru herself checked her hair and lipstick.

Deciding that she looked not one cent less than a million dollars she turned back and left the toilets. As expected Sergei was loitering not too far from the door and she only got a few steps forward before he made his move or, at least, that was what he thought that he was doing. Maybe even that was what Ru was thinking but Vixen knew differently.

"Hey, I saw you at the bar earlier," said the young Russian.

Ru stopped and smiled sweetly.

"I saw you staring at me at the bar earlier" she replied.

The man was quite a lot better built than Paul it was immediately clear from his body language that he was much surer in himself. As Ru's old drama teacher would have said, he possessed a certain assured presence but Ru found him just a little bit oily.

"Weren't you with my associate?" he asked.

"And you are?", Ru asked pretending to walk off.

"Sergei. I saw you with Paul earlier. You know the weedy black kid".

Ru stopped in her tracks and turned back to face Sergei.

"Oh yes I was...but he wasn't man enough for me if you get the picture. He's sat over in the corner, I think I was too much for him or he had a bit too much to drink".

Sergei moved closer to Ru and put his arm around her shoulder.

"I think you might find me more of, how you say, a handful?"

Ru giggled, she thought that Sergei might be correct but hopefully not in the way he was thinking.

"Come on then, you better not disappoint me", she teased.

Ru took his hand and led him into the ladies toilets and down past the cubicles to the far wall away from the door. As soon as they were there, Ru dropped her bag and Sergei pushed her up against the wall. He was quite tall but Ru still had a slight height advantage in her heels.

"You're what we would call a tsypochka, a hot chick," said Sergei as he made to kiss Ru.

As quick as a flash Ru bent down and grabbed his groin.

"That got your attention, Sergei?"

Sergei let out a nervous squeal, part in pain but mostly in fear as Ru turned him around so that it was now he who had his back to the wall.

"Now, tell me why did you kill Mikey?" she said not having to even try being authoritative as she already seemed to have his complete attention.

"What the fu… I'm going to kill you bitch!" Sergei shouted.

Ru covered his mouth with her hand and tried to knee him in the groin. At first, she missed her target and Sergei grabbed her throat but then thanks to her big boots she easily kneed him and he let go of Ru's neck. In fact, he would have doubled over but Ru held him back up against the wall. He tried to shout but not a sound got past Ru's hand.

"Shhh," she told him.

Just then the door to the bathroom burst open and two girls walked in. They saw Ru propping up a very distressed Serge and stared open mouthed at the pair.

"Would you mind just giving us 5 minutes, I just found my boyfriend cheating on me," Ru explained matter of factly.

The two girls glanced at Ru and then each other before starting laughing and hurrying outside.

"Now I'm going to ask again nicely so don't make me hurt you. Why did you kill Mikey?"

Ru removed her hand from his mouth but maintained her grip on him, keeping him tight against the wall.

"I didn't kill Mikey!" Sergei yelled.

"Well, who did? The Walkers?" Ru shouted back even louder than the Russian.

Sergei shook his head.

"No, they are money launders. Wicked men but not murderers".

"Mikey was a friend of mine and I saw you in the warehouse, the same warehouse where he was dumped in the rubbish bin outside".

"You're gonna join him when I get through with you," Sergei hollered.

"That was the wrong answer bitch!" She smiled sweetly.

Ru kneed Sergei again in the groin and he slowly slumped forward until she pulled his head back with his ponytail.

"What the hell is this mangy old thing anyway?" she mocked.

All of a sudden Sergei lunged forward and sent Ru flying into the wall of the nearest cubicle. Sergei then took a swing at her but Ru ducked and his hand smashed into the chipboard wall which stopped him in his tracks and it was of little comfort to him that he once more found himself able to scream in both pain and anger as he crouched on the floor in agony.

Ru hurried round behind him and put one arm around his neck and used the other to pull his head back. If it was put firmly in place, it would be called by many a sleeper hold which worked not by choking the victim but by cutting off the blood flow to the brain. As it was, Ru had it on loosely so that it was merely a very painful position.

"Tell me what I want to know or I'm going to break your neck, you understand!" she shouted into his ear.

Sergei had little choice but to nod his head in compliance.

"Where can I find Drew?" Ru barked.

"Drew who? You mean our boss?"

"I don't mean Drew Barrymore do I? Yes, your boss".

"Please let go of my neck I can hardly breathe. He spends most of his time at The Grove Hotel. That's where he does his business, meets his clients". Sergei replied while futilely tugging at Ru's arm.

Ru eased her grip a little so that Sergei could breathe a little easier, besides she wasn't done with him yet.

"What do you know about The Wolves?" Ru asked.

"I don't know anything. Ask Drew" Sergei stammered.

"What room number is he in?" Ru demanded

"Room 510 in the penthouse suite."

"Now listen carefully, I want you to get your phone out of your pocket and call the police on 999".

Sergei shook his head.

"You must be crazy in the head! I won't do that."

Ru quickly locked on the hold at full intensity and Sergei was soon tapping at her arms to be released. After five seconds, Ru released him and Sergei got his phone out of this pocket.

"Dial 999 and ask for Police". Ru repeated.

Sergei tapped out 999 on his phone.

"Get me the police... is this an emergency?" Sergei asked.

"Yes, it's an emergency!" Ru yelled back.

"It's an emergency," Sergei told the operator.

"Tell them to send the police, to Diamonds nightclub at the end of Market Street. Tell them that a black youth named Paul is awaiting arrest in the bar and that an unconscious Russian man in his mid 30's has attacked a woman in the toilets. Tell them they are both in a gang called The Bears".

Sergei repeated the information, only pausing once when he recited the part about an unconscious Russian.

"They are sending a car round right away, they'll be here in a few minutes" Sergei explained.

"Good now put your phone back in your pocket," Ru ordered.

Sergei pretended to do just that but simultaneously with his left arm reached up and pulled Ru's hair which caused Ru to scream. She attempted to put on the sleeper hold but such was Sergei's adrenaline and power that he lifted her up with her hanging around his neck and swung round in a circle, hitting her legs against first the cubicle wall and then the black tiled tiles on the wall of the toilet itself.

Ru couldn't understand why her hold wasn't working until she realised that by having his arm trapped between her own and his neck that he was somehow keeping the pressure off his blood flow. As Sergei pulled at her hair, Ru found herself in danger of being thrown over the Russian's head so released her grip. Sergei instinctively pulled his arm down and was about to turn to attack when Ru jumped onto his back with all her might and locked on the hold.

It sent the Russian into a blind panic and for a few seconds, he desperately pulled at Ru's hair before he began staggering into the centre of the toilet block. His yelling stopped and instead he concentrated on loosening Ru's arm from around his neck but Ru was stronger than Sergei and soon he stooped down a little. It forced Ru off his back but now with her feet firmly on the ground and his head at chest height she had a tighter hold than ever.

"I'm going to put you to sleep you scumbag and there is nothing you can do about it until you wake up in handcuffs. Next time you call Paul a scrawny kid, remember that a girl put you to sleep like a baby!"

Ru pulled him backwards into the last cubicle and Sergei flailed his arms out to the door but he couldn't prevent himself being pulled in. In fact, he couldn't stop anything at all, soon his cries were reduced to whimpers and all his aggression was soon melted away until he was meekly tapping Ru's hand until after a few seconds even that stopped and he sank to his knees. Ru kept lifted him slightly to sit on the toilet but kept the hold on tight for another ten seconds until she was convinced that he really was out for the count.

Ru felt a thrill having realised that she had quite easily knocked out the gangster and that the police would soon be here to arrest him and Paul.
"This one's for you Mikey... whether he did it or not," she said.

Ru left the cubicle and went to retrieve her bag when she heard a thud. When she returned, Sergei's head had slumped against the wall of the cubicle with his mouth wide open.

As before Ru pulled out a glove, got out her Vixen calling card and put it in Sergei's mouth between his upper lip and teeth before getting her phone out and taking a photo.

"Don't go snoring too much until the cops arrive", Ru joked as she closed the cubicle door shut behind her as best as she could.

Ru looked over to the mirrors, her hair had got a bit messed up but aside from that, had no marks at all and no-one would ever have guessed what had happened. She thought it was lucky that Sergei hadn't damaged any of her clothes otherwise she would really have got angry. As she sorted herself out, the two girls came back into the toilets and they peered round the corner to make sure everything was ok.

"My God, what happened?" asked one of them.

"He is a tit! Don't worry we sorted it out ok now, were both fine with it."

"Where is he?" the second girl asked.

"The end cubicle, best not to disturb him as he has a bit of a temper. I told him, we're through and for him to sleep on it," Ru replied.

Ru watched as the girls went into the nearest cubicles, well away from where Sergei was. Her hair back in order, she put her phone away and strode towards the door. Back in the club things had got louder, busier and darker. The whole place was throbbing and within seconds, Ru was moving anonymously through the crowds back towards the bar. She glanced over to her left to see Paul still snoozing on his seat.

Reaching the bar, she managed to get the attention of one of the barmaids.

"A Lemonade and some salt and vinegar crisps if you have any".
Ru thought she would stay and listen to the music for a while and see events unfurl when the police came. The bubbly blonde girl served her drinks and a packet of crisps.

"£4.80, please… btw that guy over there wants you to go and see him and if I were you, I'd do what he asks… if you know what's good for you".

Ru looked right over her shoulder and saw Vladimir staring coldly across the bar with his point of focus never leaving Ru for a moment.

"Great, here you go... keep the change", chirped Ru.

For a moment, Ru toyed with the idea of leaving but something inside her told her not to run but to stay here until the bitter end. If she left now, he'd only come and find her or Steve, maybe even kill them and he'd probably find a way to get his two heavies released without charge. Besides, she promised herself that she would get to the bottom of it and somewhere between the bottom and her was Vladimir.

Instead, of making for the nearest exit, Ru took a sip of lemonade and walked over to Vladimir. As she approached, the two blonde women who had been at his shoulder got up to leave. Ru sat down on a stool across the small table from Vladimir.

"I saw you go off with Paul and he hasn't come back. I saw Sergei go off with you and he hasn't come back. Are you going to take me somewhere?" he growled.

Ru smiled. "You wish."

"What's your name girl?"

"Vixen" Ru replied sash opened her packet of crisps.

"Do you even know who I am?" Vladimir asked her.

"I know who you are, I know what you are and I know what you did," Ru said without taking a break from her snack and looking the old Russian in the face as much as she could without looking away.

Vladimir leant over the table until his face was just inches from Ru's.

"What did I do? he demanded to know.

"You killed a friend and if you didn't kill him you bloody well were involved or know who did kill him", Ru said with more than a hint of anger in her voice.

"I didn't kill your friend, or, at least, I don't think I did but that doesn't mean I won't kill you".

Ru frowned, she didn't understand why everyone in this gang didn't seem to know or own up to killing Mikey. It didn't make sense.

"You were the one who came in the warehouse a few days ago aren't you? Then your stupid friend got the police round to check the bins but they didn't find anything did they. Ha-ha", the Russian guffawed.

"You're going to pay for all of this, all of you are" Ru insisted.

"You're just a girl, what are you going to do?"

"Before I beat your friend Sergei, I had him call the police, they will be here any minute. You and the other Bears are going behind bars and I don't mean the zoo!"

Vladimir let out a noise, it sounded part grunt, part snort but it was all entirely angry and disgusted.

"What have you done? You're going to pay for this!"

Just as Ru lifted her glass to take a drink, Vladimir pushed the table forward right onto Ru and sending her flying back onto the floor. Her glass of lemonade went flying, splattering her face and smashing on the ground next to where she lay. Before she could even move Vladimir grabbed a bar stool and swung it down towards Ru's head but she managed to move at the last second so it crashed into the floor.

There was a bang as the fire escape doors swung open against the back wall which caused both Ru and Vladimir to look round for a split second. It was the police.

Vladimir still crouched over Ru's head reached over for a shard of broken glass but whilst his eyes were looking in the direction of his hand, Ru took her chance suddenly raised her knees up into Vladimir's stomach which felled him in a split-second.

Ru sprung to her feet but couldn't get away as Vladimir grabbed at her boots forcing her to stamp on his hand to gain her release. Winded, from the table hit, she scurried off as quick as she could but she could hear from all the angry Russian shouting that Vladimir was just a few steps behind.

Pushing her way through the crowds, she decided to head for the stage where the live music was being performed as hopefully being the focus of the surrounding audience would dissuade Vladimir from approaching until the Police noticed what was going on.

"Out of my way, out of my way," Ru shouted as she pushed her away through the densely packed crowd.

Ru screamed as she tried to escape from Vladimir, who by now was tugging at her bag. Twice Ru wrenched it free, she was nearing the stage now and due to all the commotion the fans had separated like the parting of the Red Sea but the band seemed oblivious to it and all the while, the music continued.

Ru ran onto the stage, she didn't imagine she'd get to see Stefano so close-up and the fact that he shouted on his microphone to 'Get off my bloody set!' came as something of a shock despite her desperate predicament.

Suddenly the music stopped.

"Police, stop!" she heard.

Ru looked round and couldn't see any police or Vladimir, turning to run she ran straight into Vladimir, which sent her flying to the floor. Expecting to be pummelled, Ru looked up and to her relief she saw the group drummer bring down a drum over Vladimir's head which went through both sides rather comically before he fell motionless to the floor.

Thinking it was all part of an elaborate performance, the crowd went wild as the police arrived and arrested an unconscious Vladimir.

"Are you ok Miss?" a young Police Officer asked as he offered his hand to pull Ru up.

She took a deep breath.

"Shit yeah!"

Chapter 8

Ru didn't get home until just after 1 am and Steve had long
since gone to bed. At first the police had wanted to
formally interview her about Vladimir. However, there
had been so many witnesses that vouched for the fact that
the Russian brute had chased little Ru through the crowd
that not for a moment did anyone think that she was in any
way the instigator to all of these events. Neither did it
appear that she was implicated in the arrests of the two
other gang members which she had incapacitated. Ru
thought of the internet meme says about God, when He
does his job well, no-one even notices his existence at all.

Ru found it almost impossible to unwind after all the
action. She was still buzzing and didn't seem to be
suffering from any ill-affects so despite the late hour, she
changed outfits and went out for a quick jog twice around
the block before coming in for a hot shower before
belatedly turning in for the night.

It was impossible to sleep, she tossed one way and then the
other and then she got up and plucked her eyebrows. She
often plucked her eyebrows when driving, it took her mind
off things and she hoped by doing so now it might help her
relax.

With her eyelids finally beginning to feel if not heavy then
at least not pushed up by helium balloons she returned to
bed and thought over the events of the night while trying
to place them in the big scheme of things. Ru was pleased
that she had fared so well physically against the gangsters

whom she thought she had generally outclassed quite easily.

Ru still wasn't sure where The Bears fitted into everything, she was even beginning to have doubts that they killed Mikey after the strange denials she had encountered earlier in the evening. She hoped that she would get to the bottom of things when she paid a visit to Drew. Hopefully, he would spill the beans and if she could render him incapacitated, then as gang leader it would surely mean the end of his group.

How this all tied up with The Walkers and The Wolves, she didn't know and now she didn't quite care as she drifted off to sleep.

*   *   *

It was 10.27am, or, at least, that is what his computer clock told Steve. He hadn't heard Ru come in so at 7 am had cracked open her door to check that she was home safely. Following a breakfast of a ham and cheese omelette with a copious amount of brown sauce, Steve had gone straight on his iMac.

He decided to do a bit of research and see what information he could find on about the group that Ru had told him about, The Wolves. It didn't take long to find them on the internet, at least at a superficial level however it did take a good bit of effort to dig up some useful information on them. They weren't a big gang but they were a vicious gang and involved in anything that would make them money but predominantly they were now concentrating on distributing illegal drugs.

Apparently most if not all of the gang members are all from one extended family, possibly from Pakistan but more recently closer to home from Wolverhampton. Getting hard information on them was hard as gangs tended not to leave anything online that could get them in trouble and those outside their gang who wrote on them tended to be encouraged to remove the offending information quite quickly.

There was no specific information but there were strong rumours that they were the most vicious gang in the area and not afraid to knock people off, friends and enemies alike. The police had often tried to jail them but they had never managed to pin any convincing evidence on them. This was in no small part down to the fact that almost everyone was afraid to testify against them.

A Ru was seemingly catching up with her sleep, Steve decided to look up the other gang, The Walkers. He was quite surprised to find that they were relatively easy to locate. It seemed that they were into protection rackets and dodgy loans, the sort of people who come round and smash up flats and pummel residents to illicit payments so that nobody gets hurt, capiche? They obviously weren't too worried about getting caught as there were a number of photos of them online. Admittedly most of them they were wearing masks or scarves but it was easy enough for Steve to recognise them as being the same people who paid him a visit soon after Mikey vanished.

As Steve spent much of his time working from home on his computer, he had quite an array of software and hardware at his disposal. Steve had got his first computer in 1980, a Commodore Vic 20. Ru sometimes would joke with him when they watched re-runs of 24 on television that he had stuff that Jack Bauer would die for at CTU. Steve wasn't sure if that was entirely true but he did run through some photos of The Walkers through special software that tied into Google street view and his expectations were surpassed when he managed to find the location of where several of their photos were taken.

Steve clicked his mouse and zoomed in, they were in the middle of nowhere, well relatively speaking. Steve let out a sigh and reached for his cup of tea, it looked like they were basing themselves out of a semi-derelict cemetery from an old Victorian asylum. He thought it would, at least, appeal to Ru's sense of inner goth.

Feeling a bit stronger than in recent days, Steve decided to take a few things to the local tip or domestic waste recycling centre as the local council would call it. Ru and Steve had a few things they had each decided to get rid of and they needed some space in any case having made their recent move. Ru had already bagged up most of the things so for the first time in a long time, he grabbed his car keys and proceeded to load up the boot with bin bags. As he had to return back to the house twice, he appreciated the lack of communal stairs as anything but steady flat walking was still more than enough to make him wince in pain.

To his surprise when he returned to the kitchen the final time, Ru was up and making a brew.

"Morning Steve, you ok?", she smiled.

"Hi Ru, I'm good thanks".

He took one look at her and couldn't help but take a second glance.

"What happened with you? Get out of the wrong side of the bed this morning?" he asked.

"What do you mean?" Ru asked.

Steve walked up closer to her and touched her forehead and just beneath her right eye.

"You've got a big bruise here, Not a bad one but a big one?"

"No way, you serious?" Ru asked as she scurried into the bathroom to the mirror.

"Oh man, I have to go to work later".

Steve could hear her grumbling from the other room.

"You mean you don't remember how you did it?" he shouted through the doorway.

"No, it's ok I remember". She said.

"I remember" she repeated under her breath. "It just didn't really hurt that much when it happened".

Steve leaned against the bathroom doorframe.

"Don't tell me you fell over because I won't believe you. You've been up to something haven't you Ruby?"

Ru knew that whenever Steve called her by her full name that he had cottoned on to her. She decided to come right out and tell the truth seeing as she wanted to tell him everything anyway, even if she wouldn't have chosen this precise time to do the deed.

"I didn't go on a work-do last night. I went to a club where those guys who were in the warehouse go to." She explained.

"And they hit you?" Steve asked.

"Well one of them did, one tried to throw me through the toilets and the third just went to sleep on me".

"Are you okay? Did you call the police? Did you find anything out" Steve asked, hardly pausing for breath between the questions.

Ru nodded her head with a broad grin appearing over her face as she looked around for some foundation to see if she could hide her bruise a little.

"I did find some info out yep. Also, one of them called the police for me before I beat his ass!"

"No way?" asked Steve.

"You better believe it, bro!"

"Ru, how could you? It's so dangerous. I know you can handle yourself but I don't want anything to happen to you".

Satisfied that she had done the best of camouflaging her bruises, Ru turned round and gave Steve a hug.

"I know, I'm sorry… but I had to do something", Ru apologised.

Steve made a mental note not to give Ru too much information on what he had discovered on the computer, in fact, he had serious thoughts over whether to tell her at all.
   No point in spilling the beans if it meant she was going to get beaten up or even worse.

"Where you going, traipsing in and out of the house?" Ru asked.

"Just taking the junk down to the dump. You wanna come?" said Steve, not sure if Ru would take up the offer as it was hardly the most alluring invite she might get all day.

"If we can go via a Costa, I'll grab a soya hot chocolate," said a remarkably enthused Ru.

Steve smiled.

"Come on then".

Steve drove them both to Costa's where he stayed in the car. Getting in and out of the car was the most painful movement he could make and there seemed little point in doing so when Ru could go in and get drinks for the both of them.

A few minutes later and with Ru drinking her hot-choc and holding Steve's they were back on their way to the tip. For some reason, the tip always both fascinated and scared Steve. It was fascinating to see what people were throwing out and he often thought about where objects had been kept and who owned them as well as it being a shame that they were being thrown out. As for scary, that was purely down to the staff there that were always over officious and checking every exact item whenever he went there. He always felt that he was guilty, even when he wasn't. For sure people generated a lot of waste but he thought the staff too strict at deciding on what could be thrown where and how much one could take per visit. If he wasn't careful, he knew that he would start ranting about how it's no wonder some people just dump rubbish on the streets.

Steve parked up nearest to the containers he knew he would be using the most while trying to keep a distance from the over studious officials though not letting them suspect as such of course. It took just a few minutes to unload the car of the 6 bags in the boot. While they were going over the speed bumps, one of the bags must have split and somehow a broken table lamp had worked its way out and one of the arms of the lamp which would usually hold up the shade had become snagged on the lining of the car boot.

Steve leant over and tried to free it but couldn't see clearly enough so he ended up pulling up half the lining before he managed to do so. He was about to turn away with the lamp when he had what he would call a WTF moment.

"Here take this", he said as he gave the light to Ru.

Once she had gone, he looked more carefully. Hidden under the lining of the boot were a number of clear plastic bags of white powder.

"Shit!" he said, slamming the boot door shut as quickly as he could.

"Ru, Ru, we got to go", he shouted loudly despite the fact that she was only a few feet away.

"What is it?" she asked.

"Get in the car and I'll tell you", he replied already lowering himself back into the driving seat.

Before Ru had even closed the door, he had turned the key on the ignition and was moving away.

"Slow down Steve. What's wrong?" Ru shouted.

"There's a load of shit in the car boot".

"I know, we just went to the tip. Don't worry I can hoover it out".

Steve shook his head.

"No, I don't mean it is dirty. I mean there is a stash of drugs in the boot."

"Really?" Ru asked sounding as gobsmacked as she actually was, her mouth so wide open that as his granddad would say, her flabber was well and truly ghasted.

"Yes, several bags of it!" Steve insisted as he realised he was in excess of the 10mph speed limit and so slowed down.

"Mikey must have hidden it there. That must be why our place got smashed up. Ooh, this is getting interesting," Ru said, her brain working on overdrive to try and piece everything together.

"You mean, interesting in a 'we're both going to die' sort of way or interesting in a 'we're going to spend the rest of our natural lives in jail' sort of way?" Steve asked.

"Relax, the police will know it's not ours and the gangs aren't going to find us anymore. Besides, they already checked everywhere they could think of for the drugs."

Ru was both excited and taken aback by the discovery. Things were beginning to come together. Obviously, Mikey had hidden the drugs in Steve's car as he knew they wouldn't be found there but why was he hiding them in the first place? Ru was still musing this over when they arrived back at their new home.

"We should take it straight round to the police?" Steve said.

"We will, just not yet. Let's have a look what it is, maybe it can help us?"

"Yes Sherlock", Steve replied.

Having double checked that none of the neighbours were out and about, Ru and Steve both carried through four bags of the powder back into the house. Whilst Steve returned to lock up the car, Ru had already found a piece of paper in one of the bags. She couldn't quite make it out as she hadn't put her contacts in before they'd left home so she brought it closer up to her eyes.

The scrap of paper contained just two computer printed words
'Devil's Breath'.

"That's a funny name for a drug" she mused.

"I can't believe you brought that stuff in the house!" said Steve.

"Do you mind going on the net for a moment and look up Devil's Breath"? Ru asked.

Steve nodded and after a brief search, he had more than enough information to keep Ru happy. He called Ru over and put his finger on the screen as he read off the information.

"Devil's Breath is a powerful drug from Columbia. Its scientific name is Scopolamine and in large quantities, it is poisonous, however in small doses of a gram or less it has potent effects. Apparently the CIA used to use it as a truth serum"…

"Really?" Ru interrupted.

"If someone inhales just a small quantity of the drug it has the effect of turning them almost into a zombie. People lose their willpower and will do whatever they are told. Apparently in ancient times, the wives and mistresses of Columbian leaders used to be given this and they'd voluntarily enter burial pits only to be buried alive".

"Oh my God!" said a very shocked Ru.

"In modern times, there have been reports of people being given it and waking up having lost their internal organs mostly it is being used by thieves. In Paris recently, women have been pretending they need help only for them to blow the dust into the faces of passersby and then getting them to give them all their money or even walk them to cash machines. If anyone comes to see if the victim is ok, they get it blown in their face too. It also effects the ability of victims to form new memories which mean they don't remember what happened or who did it to them" Steve reported.

"I wonder why Mikey had it?" Ru asked.

"To make money off someone, I guess… I can't imagine he would go round robbing people in person" Steve replied.

"No wonder people are looking for it!" said Ru.

Steve logged off the computer and turned to look at the packet that Ru was holding in her hand and then up to her face to see that she had a cheeky smile on her face.

"I don't suppose I could test it on you?" she asked.
"On me? Why?" Steve stammered.

"To see if it works. It might give us an idea of what happened. It might even help us sort this whole mess out".

Steve shook his head.

"I'm sorry Ru".

"Pleeaaaaseeeee" she begged.

"I'll owe you big time," she said, pulling the cutest face she could whilst patting his arm re-assuringly.

Finally, Steve gave in.

"Ok but if you kill me you better remember this, I'll come back and get you!"

"You better not" Ru joked.

She and Steve had always been a bit psychic and she had enough to worry about without a dead Steve following her around everywhere and freaking her out in the middle of the night though it would be nice to have a friendly spirit to help with lottery wins or protecting her like some sort of guardian angel. Still, she very much preferred Steve as he was, in the land of the living.

Ru opened up the bag of the Devil's Breath and took a pinch of it between her fingers before placing it on the palm of her hand. The grains were tiny and felt more like salt than sugar but finer than both, similar to flour.

"Are you ready?" she asked.

Steve took a deep breath and slowly exhaled before nodding his head in confirmation.

Ru brought her hand towards Steve's face and blew from her mouth sending a small puff of white dust into the air. She took care to sit back slightly whilst taking hold of Steve's hand. It took only a few seconds to see Steve slightly slouch his posture and his eyes began to stare almost straight through her. It had obviously worked.

Ru wondered what to ask Steve, what could she ask that illicit a response he would not give ordinarily? Her first choice wasn't as revelatory as what it might have been.

"Are you okay Steve?"

Steve replied with a slow nod of his head.

"You know it's me yeah and I'm not going to hurt you."

Again Steve nodded his head.

"Can you make me a cup of tea, please. Also, make yourself a coffee and drink that too".

Ru watched as Steve slowly got up and walked over to the kettle. He was totally able to move around but did so in an almost robotic or zombie like way. She also knew that Steve absolutely detested coffee, even the smell of it let alone the taste of it. He would never drink it voluntarily.

Ru didn't want to risk any accidents and so walked over to the kettle and poured the boiling water herself and then offered Steve his very strong black coffee. He raised it slowly to his mouth and took a sip.

"It's nice isn't it?" Ru asked.

"Nice" replied Steve.

"Are you going to do anything I tell you?"

"Yes", he sighed.

Ru took a sip from her tea.

"Lift up your top so I can see where you got hurt".

Steve would never have usually done this as he hated people fussing around him but now he complied instantly and Ru managed to take her time to check that his injuries were healing. It was while running this through her mind that she had a brainwave. Was it possible the Bears in the club were telling the truth when they said they couldn't remember what happened to Mikey? Was it possible that the drug could have been used on someone so that they unknowingly and unwittingly killed Mikey. Or perhaps they witnessed the event but could no longer remember what happened?

As soon as she thought of the idea, Ru knew it must be true but who did what to who? She decided to test out the idea as close to real-life as she could.

"You see that big carving knife on the chopping board, Steve? I want you to go and get it and carefully bring it back to me. Don't hurt yourself".

Ru watched as Steve turned round and walked the short distance to the chopping board where a large carving knife lay from where Steve had cut off a slice of bread for breakfast. He seemed to look at it intently for a moment before bringing it back calm towards Ru.

"Very good. Now I want you to extend your left arm and lift your right arm with the knife above your head. When I say 'now' I want you to bring the knife down and cut your veins on your wrist… will you do that for me?" Ru asked gently.

"Of course, I will".

Ru went over and stood inches away from Steve as he raised the long knife above his head.

'Now!'

As soon as the sounds left Ru's mouth Steve brought down the knife towards his wrist. Despite expecting it, Ru's eyes widened in horror as she realised that Steve was about to kill himself at her command and she shot an arm out to grab Steve's forearm before he could fully bring it down.

For a second, Steve paused before trying to unsuccessfully power through.

"Steve, stop! Don't do it". Ru both commanded and begged as she raised up her other hand to place it on Steve's hand that was holding the knife.

"Give me the knife please".

Steve released his grip on the knife handle as if he had never intended to do anything but and Ru took the blade away from him, putting it safely out of reach.

"Oh man," Ru rubbed her eyes. This wasn't good.

"Did you want to kill yourself?" she asked.

Steve looked ahead blankly.

"No."

"Then why did you try and cut your wrist?"

"You told me to".

"I'm sorry Steve. I shouldn't have done that. It was bad of me."

She took him by the hand and led him back to the sofa whilst in her head she realised she should have had Steve attack her with the knife, it was wrong to potentially risk his life and not her own when he had no say in things.

"There isn't anything you're not telling me is there about this whole thing is there?" Ru asked.

Steve nodded.

"There is! Then tell me", Ru asked.

To Ru's surprise, Steve proceeded to recite everything that had happened when the gang broke into the flat that led to his hospitalisation. Even though deep inside he didn't want to say anything, he was helpless not to volunteer the information he had gleaned from his research on the internet about the gangs.

"Why didn't you tell me this earlier?" Ru asked.

"I didn't want you to get hurt. I worry about this whole situation and most of all I worry about you". His voice sounded robotic and monotonous.

Ru wasn't sure what made her ask the question she asked next but there was something in the way he spoke, something in the way he had been acting in the last few days that made her. She knew it was the wrong thing to do to take advantage of the situation but the words had just flowed from her mouth before she could stop them.

"Steve, do you trust me?"

Steve opened his mouth as if to speak but stopped. Ru wondered if the effect of the drug was wearing off and that might very be the case but as his eyes started blinking she also realised he was tiring which was a side-effect of the potent substance.

"It's ok, you can tell me?" she repeated.

"Yes, I trust you, I'd do anything for you".

His words may have been friendly but they were spoken with as little emotion as if they had been spoken by a robot.

"Listen, Steve, you're not to remember any of this whole conversation. What's more, you're going to forget all about finding the Devil's Breath and my testing it on you. And I never asked you and you never answered anything else. Do you understand?

"I do".

Ru let out a deep sigh. She felt sick, she shouldn't have asked him this. Maybe she shouldn't have done any of it, she could have killed him. Besides, he had never made any mention of it until now and everyone is allowed to like someone inside their heads.

"You've done really well but you're not safe to do anything right now. I think you're feeling exhausted so you just rest here until you're back to normal".

As quickly as Steve had brought down the knife, then he was just as soon asleep on the sofa almost as if Ru had just pressed a button. She sat and watched him for a few minutes until she could be sure he was going nowhere. It had been an interesting experiment to say the least.

"I better get these bags of Devil's Breath hidden away," she said to herself. She had to hide it in her room where no-one would find it. If nothing else, the whole experience had left her in doubt the drug was real and powerful and it most likely had got Mikey killed and it was entirely possible those who killed him didn't even know it. Thanks to Steve, she also had fresh information of who else might be involved. What a day it had been and it was still only lunchtime.

Ru was determined to get to the bottom of things.

Chapter 9

Ru didn't feel that she was looking her best. Her black eye was ripening and she felt like she had been in a fight with Mike Tyson, even if it were a fight she had won. Despite all her best efforts the bruise was showing up through her make-up. As for her hair, who knew what was going on there? It just wasn't behaving! She hadn't slept very well through the night and had spent much of it tossing and turning. Despite giving it a good wash, due to the extra time she had spent trying to conceal her bruise, she was unable to lavish the usual amount of time on her hair and quite frankly to Ru, it showed. Though whether anyone else would notice it was severely doubtful.

There was no more time to waste and she was already 10 minutes late for work. Such was the perils of an 8 am Saturday start at the Pharmacy counter. Thankfully the traffic was light on the way into Watford town centre. Ru wouldn't ever admit to speeding but admit it or not, she got to work quicker than she usually did.

Her thoughts kept straying away from her immediate work worries and more back to what she was in her head calling 'The Case'. She half expected the police to show up after the whole adventure at Diamonds Night Club but no-one had turned up. The whole thing had even been reported on the local radio station and in the Watford Observer newspaper website.

Steve hadn't suffered any visible ill effects from his inhalation of the Dragons Breath and a few hours later Ru found him to be as right as rain. What's more, and this Ru thought was a big relief, he had no idea that it had even happened or even that he had found the Devils Breath at all.

"Poor sod," Ru said to herself as she parked up.

She definitely would tell Steve all about it once all of this was over though how that would play out, Ru wasn't at all sure.

"Morning Gorgeous!"

It was Hope on Security.

"Hi Hope," Ru said as she scurried in through the broad entrance and past the metal detectors.

"Ru what happened, you look like...."

"I'm ok, just fell over in the shower", Ru said not particularly in the mood for chit-chat.

Ru continued through the vegetables area and was walking through the fresh meats when she realised that falling over in the shower might not have been the best excuse. Still, she could hardly say that she beat up three guys in a drugs gang and got her head thrown against a toilet wall in the process. Ru wasn't sure about the whole employee handbook policy but she was pretty confident that this would fall foul of some rule or regulation.

She was thankful that Nadine was away for the weekend so she only had to deal with a stand-in manager from the Luton store and he was busy on the phone when she arrived.

"Phew, I made it" Ru gleefully announced to herself, pleased that she was only 3 minutes late.

Ru threw herself straight into work, she knew that one of the old people's homes needed over one hundred repeat prescriptions sorted out and she concentrated on that. From time to time customers would come up to the counter. It was autumn and as usual, people were coming in with colds and sniffles while there was a constant flow of patients booked in for their flu vaccinations, mostly elderly and asthmatics.

Ru wasn't quite sure how she did it but at around 11 am there was a shout from her manager.

"Ru Barard, what have you done?"

Ru raised her eyebrows, finished dealing with her customer and hurried round the back.

"I don't know what you're playing at but I'm going to have to send you home?" the stand-in manager insisted.

"What do you mean?"

"I don't know what type of standards you have here but in my pharmacy, I don't expect my staff to come in looking like they've been in a fist fight or their hair looking like it's been electrocuted:.

"Look, I'm sorry but"…

Ru got cut off.

"Worst of all, you've gone and mislabelled the entire round of prescriptions for Lawns Care Home."

The manager held up some boxes as an example

"Look at that, wrong address… that one even has the date wrong. I'm sorry Ru but it's best that you go home. I'll speak to Nadine and explain the situation but I think you need to get some serious rest for a few days".

Ru brought her hands up to her eyes, she could feel the tears welling up. She'd never so much as been late in 12 years and now this happens today of all days with everything happening. She didn't bother trying to explain further, she knew it was a lost cause. Instead, she put her white jacket on its hanger, grabbed her coat and strode out towards the door, hoping the anonymity of the Saturday shoppers would provide her with covers as she sprinted out the door.

"Oh my God. Bloody, unsympathetic stand-in manager. Nadine would understand", Ru fumed.

Ru was frustrated and upset as she sat in the drivers seat of her car with her head resting forward on the wheel. She tried not to cry but things were getting tough. She sat there for several minutes before she heard a tap at the wheel.

"You ok love?"

Ru looked up to see an elderly man looking at her in a concerned way. She swept the hair out of her face and gave him a smile.

"I am thank-you for asking, though. It's very kind of you," Ru smiled back.

The old man gave her a thumbs up sign and went on his way towards the entrance. At a time like this Ru thought that only one thing could make her feel better. She reached for her phone and hit preset #3

"Hi is that Kirstie at Hobb Salon? Yes, it's Ru. Can I make an appointment?… Yeah, I can make it in 15 minutes, just try and stop me. See ya!"

*   *   *

Ru parked up her car in their new front driveway and got out. She whipped out her iPhone and flicked on the camera in selfie mode as she admired herself from head to toe but mostly her head or rather hair.

"Shit girl, you're looking hot!" Ru complimented herself.

It had taken most of the afternoon but the £125 had been money well spent. Besides, Ru thought it would help her create a new identity around Vixen. Gone was her long smooth and straight jet black hair. Now she was sporting a slinky new look, still black but with lashings of dark red lowlights amongst her now wavy hair. As she knew one of the stylists there, she had also got a special deal to have a gel nails manicure and she found herself repeatedly checking herself out not short drive back home.

"I like it a lot, Vixen is going to be such a bad-ass". Ru had decided that if she wasn't able to work at her paid job, then she would put all her efforts into her unpaid one and make Vixen the baddest looking vigilante this side of the silver screen.

She closed the car door and opened up the house front door. She hardly got a step inside when Steve entered the hallway with a knife.

"Shit, Ru, what happened", he stammered.

"Oh man, I'm sorry. I should have texted".

"You look..." his voice trailed off as he stared at Ru's hair.

"Hot?" Ru asked

"Err... yeah, I guess so", Steve replied followed by a nervous laugh.

"It's part of the new me. Work sent me home for a day or two so I decided to cheer myself up a bit. I hope you like it".

Steve nodded and went back in the kitchen to put the knife down.

"Is everything ok with work?" he shouted through the doorway.

"It's all ok, just some tit being an arse. Do you mind putting the kettle on please?"

Ru went straight to the bathroom to admire her new look and she liked what she saw.

"Tea's ready!" she heard shouted through the door.

Ru went into the living room, Steve was at work on his computer.

"You working on a book or an article?" She asked.

"Neither, I'm on eBay actually bidding for a bladed instrument".

Ru shook her head in mock disgust.

"No way! Just say sword or dagger or spear. You already have half a dozen under your bed what you getting this time?"

Ru didn't exactly get Steve and his antique weapons collection, for someone who wouldn't hurt a fly, he sure had lots of options of how to go about doing so if only he weren't such a softie.

"A WW1 bayonet."

Ru took a sip of tea.

"Look I don't mind you putting up those 3 samurai swords on the wall, even the Zulu shield and spear but not a bayonet, that's disgusting". Ru said forcefully.

"Maybe if I get a rifle for it to fit in?" Steve asked.

"No! Anyway, how you feeling now?", Ru said 'No' emphatically enough that she left in no doubt there would be no bayonet ordering happening today.

Steve smiled.

"I'm ok I guess. I like the new place, I'm getting less sore by the day and my headaches have gone. I'll be as good as new soon so long as I don't get another kick-in," he explained.

"That's really good. Listen, I'm going to get changed and then I'll make us a snack".

She hurried through to the bathroom, the shout of Steve telling her that she better not be going out to the club again registered in her ears but not in her actions.

She put on a dark maroon low cut dress which she thought went with her hair. A simple pair of boots finished the look, they didn't have the highest of heels but they were few boots in the known world that were shinier than these.

Back outside, she found Steve had logged off his computer and was sat watching WWE on the television. He wasn't actually in the Roman Reigns fan club but enjoyed watching the bouts well-enough. Steve was more a fan of Brock Lesnar but for entirely different reasons than Ru with her Roman infatuation.

Ru went to the kitchen and made some sandwiches and got a family packet of crisps out of the pantry and poured out glasses of Tango from the 2-litre bottle in the fridge. She felt bad at what she was going to do and because of that she vowed never to do it again, to Steve at least, but Ru knew he wouldn't let her go out tonight while now she was freed from work, she felt more like kicking-ass than ever.

She got two of Steve's sleeping tablets and emptied the powders into his glass of drink. Once they had suitably dissolved, she took his plate and drink through before returning for her own. Neither of them really ever drank fizzy drinks so she hoped that the relative novelty of it would encourage him to drink up.

Steve downed his sandwiches but as the pair had only recently had a cup of tea, he obviously wasn't as thirsty as he would have been. Every sip he took Ru stole a glance at him. For some reason, Ru felt more and more overcome by guilt and she decided that if she couldn't own up to things, she, at least, had to explain a little.

"Listen, Steve, I got to tell you. I'm beginning to work out how we can get to the bottom of all this, how we can get justice for Mikey".

"By calling the Met and letting their capable detectives handle this?"

The tone of his voice was just sarcastic enough for Ru to realise he was joking.

"No, listen. I've found out about this guy Drew, he is in charge of the gang from the warehouse... the ones we think killed Mikey."

Steve nodded his head.

"Well I want to take him out and I don't mean for a pizza," Ru explained softly.

"No Ru, you can't kill him!" Steve said, completely misreading the situation.

"Ok, I don't want to kill him but I was to sort him out and get to the bottom of things", she explained.

"And what about the others? The other gangs?" Steve asked.

"I'll, I mean we'll take care of things one step at a time".

Steve let out a long and deep sigh.

"Are you ok Steve?" Ru asked.

"No Ru, just no. Look, you got beat up last time!"

"I didn't get beat up. I got my face thrown into the wall in the process of my beating up three guys."

Ru spoke as calmly as she could to avoid escalating the situation but it was too late and Steve leapt out of the sofa and strode over to the front door and turned the lock.

"You're dressed up. I know you want to go out tonight but I'm not going to let you," insisted Steve

Steve turned to see Ru get up off the sofa.

"Don't be like that. Besides, do you really think you could stop me," Ru asked

"I'd do my best, to stop you getting killed".

Steve stopped and started rubbing his eyes with his fingers.

"It's ok Steve, forget it, I'm not going back to the club tonight. Look you're getting dizzy again. Let's get you back on the sofa and we'll just watch Dr Who or something", she acquiesced.

Ru ran over and helped him back to the sofa, she knew very well that Steve wasn't just dizzy and she hoped if she were kept him occupied, he wouldn't have time to figure anything out. She sat him down on the sofa and plonked herself down right next to him.

"Are you going to sleep during wrestling! Disgusting" she teased.

Steve shook his head but Ru knew his dilated pupils and sagging head told a different story.

"Why did I get my hair done if you're just going to nod off?!?" she playfully continued.

Ru turned the volume down a bit on the tv. She was surprised how much longer Steve had lasted than Paul. For a baddie, Paul was such a dweeb.

She watched as first his head would droop forward and then quickly rise back until after a minute or two his whole body began to sag.

"You poor thing, why don't you lay down flat", Ru got up and lifted Steve's legs up onto the sofa before easing his head down.

She wondered if Steve had cottoned on to her plan even at a subconscious level as his heavy eyes peered out stubbornly at her.

"Don't fight it, just go to sleep," she soothed.

She ruffled his hair with her fingers and her soothing actions did the trick. For a few minutes, his breath remained shallow but soon deepened until it almost sounded like snoring.

"I'm not going to do this again, I know you just don't want me to get hurt and I really appreciate it. I've got work to do though and I'm doing this in part to make sure you don't get hurt", she spoke softly and apologetically as if he could hear every word, even though Ru knew this to be impossible.

Knowing that she still had a little time to kill, Ru perched herself on the end of the sofa and watched the end of the wrestling. Deciding it was time to go, she put the TV remote control in Steve's hand. It was really unlikely he would wake up but if he did, then Ru knew he'd just presumed he fell asleep on the sofa as normal.

She picked up her car keys. She had a date with Drew, even if he didn't yet know it.

Chapter 10

It was a 20-minute drive to The Grove Hotel. Ru hadn't
been there before but she had always wanted to visit.
Besides the fact that it didn't seem to make much sense for
her to stay in a hotel in the same town as where she lived,
there was the small matter of the cheapest room coming in
at around £300 per night.

The hotel was well known to serve an exclusive clientele
whether they be foreign dignitaries, sports teams, movie
actors working at the nearby Leavesden Studios or just
those with more money than they knew what to do with.
Ru thought that she would fit in fine just so long that she
didn't have to pay any bills but she wondered if the hotel
even had a clue about the gangsters using their penthouse
suite as a base of operations. Probably they did but just
turned a blind eye. Who is really going to turn away
customers that pay thousands of pounds per night,
providing no-one gets roughed up in the Reception area
the answer is likely that no-one is.

She felt a mix of excitement tinged with a little
apprehension and this was played out in the nervous
feeling she felt in her stomach and she almost didn't stop at
the red lights on the dual carriageway into town. While
calling herself an 'idiot' in her head, she checked in the
mirror to make sure her hair was ok. Even in the car
interior lit only by headlights of the cars behind, her
brilliant crimson ends of her hair were visible and she
couldn't help but play with them with her fingers until her
tranquility was rudely disturbed. Her thoughts about

visiting The Grove were temporarily put on hold when a car pulled up alongside her own and started honking their horn. Ru tried to ignore it until the shouts of the driver egged on by a car full of equally rowdy young men made her look round.

"Oi, you're well fit. You wanna come round to ours?" asked a skinny, blonde youth who had lowered his window.

"You wish boys, I'm off to The Grove".

"Don't be like that, we got beers, drugs. Everything you'd want", the teenager argued.

"Do you have any guys that are a lot hotter than you lot?" Ru laughed.

"Screw you!" said the frustrated driver who Ru saw couldn't be much more than a student in a severely souped up but ultimately lame looking Ford Focus.

"Ha, you wish!" Ru replied, pressing the button to close up the window.

She could hear the driver in the car adjacent to her revving the engine so she knew what was coming and she was ready for it. The lights turned amber and then green, Ru felt like in the mood to play so she put her foot down. The tyres on the car beside her screeched away but Ru played it cool, she knew it wasn't even a contest in her Audi turbo. Instead just paced herself so that she was a few inches off her opponent no matter how fast he drove but encouraging him that if he went quicker, then he might just win.

30 mph, 40mph, 50mph, the needle on the speedo moved ever more clockwise as they roared down the A41, which was thankfully almost deserted of traffic given the speed they were increasing to.

"I'm through playing with these bastards," she said to herself as she lowered the window again and slightly slowed her acceleration. The windows of the other car were still open with at least two yobs shouting abuse at her, encouraged by the deception that they were gaining on Ru.

Ru knew that there was a 50mph speed limit coming up at the traffic lights as they were now entering a built up area, why did she think the boys wouldn't remember.   They were nearly at 70mph when Ru let the Ford Focus draw level.

"Say cheese you twats!", she yelled.

Ru chose not to listen to the replies as she slammed on her brakes just in time and she watched the car full of yobs roar ahead in apparent triumph. A second later was the double flash of the speed camera, she saw the car brake lights come on but it was too late and with any luck they were exceeding the speed limits so much someone would lose their licence.

It was a great start to the evening, Ru tapped her nails on the steering wheel and smiled.

"I'm such a bitch!"

She saw the car in front turn left at the roundabout while Ru headed straight on up the hill and a few minutes later she soon found herself at the entrance to The Grove. The estate of the hotel must have been magnificent as she could only just make out the lights of the hotel on the horizon as she followed the single track driveway round in an elegant curve and over an old stone humped back bridge before parking up a short distance from the hotel reception.

She put her car interior lights on and made one last check. She noticed part of her eyebrow was out of place so she got her tweezers out and with a quick pull, she was all set.

It was chilly outside and as she wasn't wearing a jacket it made her stride across the car park even faster than she normally did in her boots. A doorman who was coming out to prepare for a limousine that was parking up opened the door for her.

"Good evening Madam."

Ru smiled back.

"Evening".

The Reception area of the hotel was quite large but not as plush as she might have expected, it being decorated in a modern and contemporary style which didn't really fit with her expectations of a country house. Not that she had a great deal of experience with these things beyond the

Antiques Roadshow and Escape To The Country on a Sunday afternoon slumped in front of the television.

She walked over to the Reception Desk where she was met by a young, friendly Chinese looking lady smiling up across the table.

"Hi, I'm here to see Drew?"

"Drew who?" the receptionist replied.

For a moment, Ru thought she was trying to be funny but then she realised she wasn't but also that she didn't know his surname.

"You know Drew. The guy in the Penthouse suite".

The receptionist nodded affirmatively.

"Oh yes of course, why don't you speak with my colleague there at the Concierge, he deals exclusively with Mr Drew's clientele."

Ru nodded a thanks and walked a few feet over to the Concierge where a chubby South African sounding man stopped talking to another similarly proportioned but taller man in mid-sentence and leered at her sleazily.

"I'm here for Drew", Ru instructed.

"I thought she wasn't due here for another two hours?" said one of the men

"Oh I'm a little surprise for him," said Ru with a pout that was so hot it would melt chocolate.

"Oh man, how come my surprises are like standing in dog crap in the park and Drew's are all like her?", the concierge remarked.

"You couldn't afford me anyway. Now you going to show me up or shall I tell Drew that you're causing trouble?"

Ru spat out the words as if they were poison as she revelled in the part she was playing.

"Ooh, Drew's going to like her. She's got a bit of fight in her" said the English sounding guy who the Concierge had been talking to.

"I'm Sebastian, I am one of Drew's associates. I'll take you up to him. Follow me".

Ru turned and followed Sebastian round the corner.

"We not going up in the lift?" She asked.

"Oh we are but the Penthouse has got its own private and secure lift. Drew doesn't like unexpected disturbances", Sebastian explained.

"Oh that's good," Ru said a little too excitedly as she knew it would give her time and space to do her work.

"Good?" Sebastian asked.

"I mean it's good that we won't be disturbed... if you know what I'm saying!" Ru replied in a more measured but sexy tone.

A few feet on from the main lift was a smaller one, just big enough for three or four people rather than the usual 8 or 10 that most other lifts could house. Sebastian pressed the button and the doors rolled open instantly and silently.

Sebastian walked in first and Ru followed a second later. Noticing that Sebastian is eying her up, Ru flashes him a quick smile. Her mind was racing quickly. She didn't just want to beat Drew, she had to get information out of him and she imagined that might be hard to do. Harder still with reinforcements in the room or the suite next door. Everyone she encountered between here and Drew had to be neutralised, figuratively speaking.

She didn't have to wait long before an opportunity presented itself. Sebastian smiled and reached behind him. The lift rumbled to a halt.

"It's just you and me babe, we're not going to be disturbed here", he said.

"We're not? Really? This is my lucky day!" Ru replied with a twinkle in her eye.

Sebastian took a step towards Ru and reached out his arm. Ru quickly grabbed it and held it behind his back catching him completely by surprise but before he could do anything she took his body and rammed him head first into the aluminium wall panelling.

Sebastian groaned but he didn't go down.

"You wanted a bit of fun, I'll give you a bit of fun" Ru shouted as she jumped up so her hands could grab the light fittings before clamping her thighs down around Sebastian's neck.

Instantly he tried to wriggle free as he shouted threats of how Ru was going to be a dead woman. Neither the threats or the wriggling seemed to have much of an impact on Ru, who if anything locked on an even tighter grip.

Sebastian tried to pull himself free but nowhere in the confines of the lift were out of reach of Ru's legs and he found himself slowly choking with no way to breathe. His only recourse was to firmly dig his fingers into Ru's thighs which in the grand scheme of things barely made an impact on Ru and soon he was reducing to pitifully tapping her legs for release.

"I hate guys who are all talk and no action", Ru said as she squeezed his neck that not only was it impossible for him to breathe but he as almost being held up by her as his legs began to give way.

It was almost too good to be true, Ru thought. A private and confined space with no escape. After about 30 seconds Sebastian began to sag and as Ru kept a tight grip on the lighting it only had the effect of weakening him more quickly as all the pressure fell on his neck. Ru let go of the lights and Sebastian almost fell down like a sack of potatoes. If he hoped he was going to escape, he must have quickly realised there was no hope as Ru kept his head securely between her legs and even after both her feet were firmly on the floor.

"Easy-peasy," she said to herself as he fell unconscious. Ru though didn't move for a good 30 seconds as she wanted to make sure he didn't make a Hulk Hoganesque recovery. Finally, she let go and took a step back. For a moment, Sebastian's head tilted backwards before his body fell face forward to the carpeted floor at her feet.

"Didn't your mother tell you to be careful with who you get into a lift with?" she said as she watched Sebastian lay motionless on the floor.

Ru took a moment to compose herself and check the mirrored wall of the elevator that she hadn't ruined her look. Then she reached into her handbag and pulled out a sleeping tablet.

"Euu, you've made a real mess of yourself Seb".

Sebastian had saliva all over his face but as Ru was sure he would only stay unconscious for 15 minutes she had no choice but to gingerly pull open his drool covered jaw and stick the tablet inside.

"That's so you don't get any ideas of walking out on me" Ru joked.

"Right, lets's get down to business".

Ru pressed the button labelled 'Stop/Start" and after a second the lift resumed its progress upwards and after a few seconds, there was a ding of a bell and the doors opened.

Ruby poked her neck round the corner to check that the coast was clear. The lift opened out onto corridor a black granite floor with dark oak panelled walls along both sides decorated with a gold trim. Periodically along the hallway were both downlighters and up lighters and she was able to see a number of doors leading off the corridor on the left. To the right was a small alcove which Ru peered in and saw what appeared to be a cleaners cupboard. It was full of mops, hoovers and cleaning materials but there was just enough room to store something else.

"Cool," Ru said to herself as she figured out what to do next.

Obviously having the lift return down to the lobby with an unconscious Sebastian on the floor wouldn't do much to help her chances and so she picked grabbed hold of his hands and started dragging him along the floor, out of the lift and onto the smooth mosaic floor. Almost as soon as they were out of the lift, the doors closed and Ru saw on the indicator that it was returning to the ground floor.

"Come on Ru, sort yourself out," she chided herself. It was vital that she get a move on lest anyone else appear and find her in a compromised situation.

Ru found it relatively easy to knock Seb out but pulling him even along the smooth floor was another matter. One thing was for sure, he was going to wake up with a sore arse in the morning.

Ru hoped that the door was actually unlocked but then someone who pays thousands of pounds for a room each night is hardly likely to go into the cleaners cupboard to steal an extra toilet roll. She let go of Sebs hands and watched as they fell quickly by his side before trying the door handle. Thankfully it was unlocked and she pulled the motionless body inside. It was a little cramped so Ru has to sit Sebastian against the back wall and push his knees up under his chin in order to be able to close the door.

"Night-night!" she giggled.

'Ding', the lift doors opened and with Ru and two tall, well-built men stepped out. One was wearing a suit and looked like he had just come back from a job interview whilst the other was wearing more semi-formal clothes however he would still be considered as being smartly dressed if he wasn't stood next to his suited companion.

Ru swore in her head as they looked round to the right and she did her best to look casual.

"You look a bit dressed up to be a cleaner", said the suited man as soon as he set eyes on Ru.

Ru smiled nervously.

"Oh no, I'm not a cleaner. I'm a little lost. I met a guy over a drink or two down in the party and I'm sure he said his room was here".

"No, I don't think so. Just three rooms up here and Drew and I have been in a meeting until now".

Ru started walking towards them with her arm outstretched and with just a little bit of acting, managed to trip herself up sending herself falling almost at men's feet.

"Sorry, had a bit to drink", she apologised whilst hoping the whole event didn't seem overly staged.

Neither man was quick to help but finally the suited individual reached over and helped Ru to her feet.

"Thank-you, sorry about that!" Ru said as she pretended to compose herself.

"Nathan, why don't you take care of the young lady and meet me back in my room in half an hour or so".

"Sure thing boss", Nathan spoke with a broad grin as Drew was already walking towards his penthouse suite.

Ru tried her best to look blurry eyed and more than a little drunk, it wasn't easy given that she never really drank and had never been properly drunk due to an allergy to alcohol.

"Wow, you have must have big muscles under your shirt."

"I do work out a lot yeah, I need to in my line of work", replied Nathan.

"Are you the wrestler Roman Reigns?"

Nathan laughed.

"No, I'm not. Hell, you're wasted aren't you. Why don't you come with me and I'll help you find your friend".

"Sure, why not. Is he inside?".

"Well we can have a look can't we?" said Nathan.

Ru walked alongside Nathan, who though not much taller than herself was very well built. Even in the 20 feet to his bedroom door, Ru pretended to stumble and this time, Nathan was ready to catch her. She wanted to ensure that he was totally underestimating her before she struck for Ru most definitely had to get him out of the picture if she was going to get Drew to talk.

Nathan opened the door and let Ru in first before following her inside. Ru loved the room with a four post bed and the most amazing drapes around the window. Even Nathan was hot, if only he weren't an evil henchman she thought.

While Nathan was taking off his suit jacket, Ru quickly reached into her handbag and retrieved two sleeping tablets. It occurred to her that Nathan was fully expecting to sleep her with and though she could risk a fight, it is likely that Drew would hear next door and she didn't want any of that. She also made a mental note that being a chemist there must be a quicker way to nonviolently incapacitate someone than using tablets and that she would have to look into other methods should she get through tonight in one piece.

Quickly she put the container back in her bag and then rushed two tablets into her mouth and tried to position them under her tongue taking great care most of all not to swallow them.

She hurried over to Nathan, who was taking off his tie and looked into his brown eyes before taking hold of his cheeks and kissing him as passionately as she could. At first, Nathan tried to pull away but Ru knew the tablets were still in her mouth so she scooped them onto her tongue and quickly placed them under his. Only when she knew that Nathan was gagging for air did she finally let him go. Nathan instinctively swallowed and if he noticed the small tablets, he certainly didn't let on.

"Shit girl, that was some kiss".

"Wasn't it!" Ru giggled sweetly.

"Do you mind if I go quickly to the bathroom so I can make myself ready for you?"

Nathan shook his head.

"Be my guest".

Ru walked slinkily to the bathroom and closed the door behind her. Never had she seen such a beautiful bathroom, made entirely or Italianate marble with an ornate mirror to die for.

"Wow, Nathan loves himself… can't blame him, though". Ru mused.

In the corner was Jacuzzi, she really wanted to try it out. She wanted to buy herself as much time as possible for the tablets to take effect but just jumping in the Jacuzzi might be pushing her look.

Something inside her head made her wonder how she had quite got into this position. She didn't even like to look at herself in the mirror, let alone have some sleaze ball, albeit quite a hot one, see her like this. Ru almost thought she was losing her nerve and then she reminded herself, she wasn't Ru at least not right this minute. She was Vixen and Vixen does whatever is needed to get the job done. If men were stupid and helpless enough to fall for her, then that's exactly what she will do to them in order to get what she wants.

Vixen was like a mask, an alter-ego that Ru could slip in and out of both physically and mentally. She undressed slowly and checked her face was still looking good, even Vixen was into keeping her appearances she decided.

She was glad that she had worn her matching white lace bra and underwear rather than her Wolves FC matching set. For a moment she admired herself in the mirror, her long wavy hair cascading over her shoulders.

"I'd do you a favour girl!" she giggled.

She opened the bathroom door and walked as sexily and seductively as she could and saw Nathan undressed on the bed. Ru was a little disappointed that he wasn't in anyway shape or form asleep. Having sex was out of the question, of course, even the thought made her shudder.

"Fuck!" she said to herself.

"That's what you're here for isn't it?" Nathan commented.

Ruby wrapped herself around one of the four posts of the bed like a cat.

"Those are a mean set of claws on you".

Ru smiled and tapped her nails on the bedpost.

"Come on, let's stop messing around, I got to go see Drew in 20 minutes". Nathan growled.

"Ok, but don't say I didn't warn you!" Ru exclaimed whilst still trying to work out what to do next.

Ru climbed abreast of Nathan and began to kiss him once more though not as intensely as when she had a reason for doing so.

Then she brought up her forefinger to his lips.

"So you like my nails do you. I hope you like this."

She ran her fingers down his neck, across his chest and down to his well-conditioned stomach. Nathan closed his eyes or rather they flickered, Ru knew it wasn't just her touch that was having an effect on the gangster.

Ru then sat atop his stomach in one single motion but at the same time, Nathan's eyes opened wide.

"Wait a minute, you couldn't have gone in our lift by mistake, you'd have had to get past the Concierge. You never even said your name".

"Shhh, don't talk when we can make out", Ru purred.

It was useless, though, Nathan realised something was amiss.

"What's happening, how come you're not drunk anymore. How come I am?" he thundered.

Ru moved quickly and pinned Nathan's arms under her legs while sitting firmly on his chest. He could kick his legs around but not very much else.

"Relax, I'm not hurting you, just sending you to sleep. Of course, when you wake up you'll be in prison. In 15 minutes you'll be sleeping like a baby and I'll knock on Drew's door and kick his ass like I'm kicking yours."

"You can't do this to me. Dre...."

Ru slapped her hand down over Nathans' mouth. He quickly turned his head left and right but couldn't get away from her hand. Then Ru felt a sharp pain, Nathan had tried his best to bite her.

"You sleazebag!" She muttered under her breath before digging her nails into his chest until he let her go.

"Shhh, just look into my pretty face and big beautiful eyes".

She released her hold only slightly so he could breathe, Ru had absolutely no intention of killing anyone.

Feeling his kicking subside, V removed her hand from Nathans' mouth.

"I totally owned you didn't I Nathan. My name is V by the way".

Nathan's only response was repeated but ever slowing blinking of his eyes. Ru felt like having fun.

"You like my claws so I tell you what if you can do what I ask then I'll let you go. Despite all your muscles I bet my beautiful long nails are stronger than you and can put you out for the count. I'm going to close your eyes and If you can open them I will let you go", Ru said playfully.

Ru stretched out her forefinger and index finger and using just her nails held Nathans eyelids shut. For a moment she could feel them straining to move so, she counted slowly

"One… two… three…four…five".

Gently she took away her fingers but Nathan wasn't going anywhere.

Ru checked her hand to see that it wasn't cut from when she was bitten. Her hand was red but the skin hadn't been broken.

"Now we've taken care of the mice, let's go see the cat".

Taking her time, Ru pranced back into the bathroom and got dressed. Having checked that she was still looking good, she reclaimed her handbag and retrieved one of V's calling cards placing it squarely on the middle of Nathans' chest right next to where she had scratched him.

Pleased with herself, she finally headed to the door and switched off the lights.

"Sweet dreams", Vixen had claimed another victim.

Chapter 11

The corridor was just as she had left it perhaps 20 minutes earlier. There wasn't a sound to be heard from Drew's room and they were so high up that Ru guessed no-one on the lower floors would hear anything that happened up here.

"In The Grove, no-one can hear you scream", Ru smiled to herself.

Drew's door was more opulent than the others, and, in fact, was made up of two dark oak doors with a handle on each of them that looked gold even if they weren't. Taking a breath, she knocked twice on the right door. The doors here sounded more substantial than the walls of their old flat, Ru thought.

"Come on in Nathan, the doors unlocked," said a voice from inside.

Ru opened the door to the suite. She wasn't sure whether to sneak in or stride in but then she remembered she was V and V marched into rooms, not afraid of anyone.

As she entered the room, she was amazed to see how big and open it was with gorgeous antique furniture around the bed and more contemporary furnishings elsewhere which included a 100-inch ultraHD TV which was playing with the volume down.

"I'm just taking a slash Nathe, I'll be out in a moment," Drew shouted out through the bathroom door.

Ru couldn't believe just how lush the whole penthouse was decorated. It must cost a fortune to live here, all illegally gained too she was absolutely certain.

Ru walked past the bathroom and was about to put down her bag on the table when she was sent flying through the air against the back wall.

"Just for your information, next time Nathan doesn't ever knock on the door".

It was Drew and he rushed over and picked and grabbed Ru by her arms and three times rammed her back into the wall. She barely knew what was happening and was winded from the unexpected fall.

"Who are you?" he demanded to know.

Ru smiled at him which though it wound up Drew further. Truthfully, however, it was all she could do in a way of response.

"Tell me, I want to know!" Drew screamed just inches in front of her, sending a spray of spit showering her face.

"My name is Vixen and I'm here to get justice for my friends." Ru wheezed.

"Vixen, so you're that girl whose been causing so much trouble. By the time I get through with you, you'll wish that you had never caused me the trouble," Drew threatened.

With that, Drew pulled Ru up, lifted her off her feet and threw her across the floor. She landed heavily and cluttered into the wall of the bathroom. Ru wasn't just dazed she knew she was in danger of leaving the penthouse in a box and from deep inside her, somewhere she managed to make a real concerted effort to fight back. When Drew neared she kicked out with her right leg, catching him square on the chin which sent him reeling backwards.

Seizing her moment as best as she could, Ru climbed to her feet but was met by an incoming punch to the face. She blocked one blow with her arm but didn't see the other and was again sent sprawling, her face throbbing with pain. Again, Drew grabbed hold of Ru and swung her against a wall almost as if she was a toy. In a heap in the corner, she still had the wherewithal to She grabbed hold of a light fitting to stop herself falling over only to be struck by a wooden chair across her back. Unable to defend herself she staggered two steps back before Drew lunged at her, grabbed her hair and swung her onto the bed.

Unlike Nathan, Drew had no intention to do anything but kill Ru and with her lying breathless on the bed, he picked up a pillow and thrust it firmly across her face. Ru instinctively writhed around, kicking her legs up wildly but they could find no target.

Her lungs were burning, she couldn't see anything or feel anything but for the pillow onto of her face. Her right hand managed to find his but she could do nothing to get him to ease his grip.

"I'm going to kill you, you bitch. Did you think I was going to fall for your looks like those idiots at the club? You've lost me a lot of money and the pigs are sniffing around like crazy", Drew explained as calmly as if this were a very mundane event in his life.

Ru's panic turned to terror and her terror to desperation as she began to choke. Her left arm splayed around looking for something, anything to grab hold of. Then she felt something with the tips of her fingers, Ru thought it must be some sort of bedside light. She stretched as far as she could and manage to wrap her fingers around the pole but she couldn't move it. She tried but then for a second she blacked out.

On the other side of the pillow, Drew could barely hear a whisper but Ru let out a scream, she was back and with nothing left in her reserves her fingers tightened around the lamp and she lifted it off the table and swung it towards Drew, striking him firmly across the side of his head. He let out a groan and immediately fell backwards, his hand still holding the pillow tightly, pulled it away from Ru's face and the air flooded back into her lungs.

Ru couldn't move, she just lay still wheezing and taking the deepest of breaths that seemingly did little to satiate her need for air. She wanted to take the fight to Drew who lay semi-conscious just inches away but all she could do was try and breathe.

She looked over and saw that she had shattered a heavy, large Rennie Mackintosh inspired glass light shade over Drew. She clenched her abs and sat herself up.

"Now listen to me bitch. You're into business and business is all about supply and demand. I'm going to demand information and you're going to supply it", Ru prodded her finger into Drew's face as if she were reprimanding an unruly child.

Ru clambered off the bed and scurried over to her bag to retrieve some cable ties which she planned to tie Drew up so she could question him. Her brain though was slowed by a lack of oxygen and didn't process the fact that Drew was now moving off the bed too and she was genuinely surprised to see him standing before her when she turned round.

He swung another punch at her but missed, Ru hit back with one of her own that connected but it wasn't very strong and merely stopped him in his tracks. He attacked her again and, this time, punched her in the stomach.

If Drew thought he would wind Ru, he had another thing coming. Ru knew he could have punched her like that all day as she had Abs like iron.

"I have more muscle in my tummy than you do in your arm you arsehole," she screamed.

Ru once more punched Drew clean in the face and this time sent him back against the dressing table. Now acting out of desperation himself, Drew pulled open the top drawer of the desk and whisked out a knife.

Ru saw what he was doing but wasn't able to stop him and he lashed out with it slashing Ru on her arm just below her right shoulder. She grabbed his hand and slammed it against the wall forcing him to release the weapon and then head butted him. Quickly she followed up and kicked him in the groin. As Drew stood doubled up helplessly, Ru took hold of his left arm and wrenched it back. There was a crack and a yell which made even Ru wince.

She let him go and as Drew stood wailing, pitifully she stood up, took a breath and punched him with all her might in the face. Drew fell back to the floor before a second later slumping to the floor.

"Thank fuck for that" Ru squeezed out between deep breaths.

She walked over to the dressing table and pulled out a chair. Then she dragged Drew round the bed and pulled him up onto the seat before taking out some cable ties. Not only did she tie his arms together behind his back but also secured his feet to the legs of the chair. He wasn't going to go anywhere and would no doubt feel the pain of his broken arm from the moment that he regained consciousness which might encourage him to be more cooperative in answering her questions.

Her own body beaten black and blue, Ru was content to rest for a few minutes until Drew came to. She went into the bathroom and had a look at where her arm had been slashed. It only looked like it was a minor cut and as she washed it over with cold water she counted herself incredibly lucky that she had made it through the last 15 minutes.

She wondered if she had been getting complacent or whether, as the boss, Drew was just more desperate not to lose than any of those under him. Either way, she promised herself to be more aware of her surroundings in the future.

When she returned to the bedroom, Drew was just waking up and his head was rolling from side to side. She walked over and yanked his head up by his hair

"Now that you've killed me you bastard, I wonder if you're ready to talk?"

"And if I don't?" Drew yelled.

"Then I am going to bloody kill you like you did to my friend", Ru fumed.

Drew shook his head.

"What the hell have you done to my arm?" He screamed.

"I think it got broke, you know when you stabbed me." Ru hit back.

"Right start talking."

"Screw you", Drew spat out at Ru both figuratively and physically.

"Drew, Drew, Drew. That was the wrong answer bitch."

Ru walked across the room and picked up the knife which Drew had previously attacked her with. She toyed with the blade and admired its sharp perfection holding one hand on the handle and touching the point with a finger.

She walked back to Drew and brought the knife blade up to his neck pushing it into his skin but not so much that it broke.

"Ok, Ok!" he flustered.

"What do you know about The Walkers?" Ru asked, staring deep into his eyes from just a few inches away.

"The Walkers are nothing to do with me," Drew furiously denied.

"They came in and beat my roommate to within an inch of his death looking for something" Ru explained

"I said, they're not my responsibility.

"You still know more about them than I do! So tell me now!" Ru said as she pushed the blade of the knife deeper into his neck.

"That guy Mikey, he owed them money. The Walkers are loan sharks, gamblers. Mikey owed them a heap of money. I mean a mountain of money".

"Where can I find them? Come on, they're not in your organisation, what do you care what happens to them?" Ru asked.

"They're small fry. You've got them spooked and what with the police on their tail... they are probably holding out where they generally go to when they turn chickenshit".

"Which is where exactly?" Ru asked.

"The old cemetery at Leavesden Asylum." Drew pro-offered.

"So where does your group come into it... The Bears. I heard those Russians in the warehouse, I found Mikey dumped outside".

Drew shook his head.

"You're not going to kill me!" Drew smiled.

Ru pushed the knife harder into his neck but Drew refused to answer the question.

"Damn it!" Ru screamed.

She removed the knife from Drew's neck and plunged it deep into his left thigh sending a squirt of blood up into the air. Drew screamed out like a wounded animal which shocked Ru more than the fact that she had stabbed him in the first place.

It took over a minute before Drew quit wailing as Ru practically laughed in his face.

"Shit woman. Mikey owed us drugs. We paid him a lot of money for a new type of drug and he went and squandered it on gambling. That's what we had to do with it. He was playing off all the gangs, trying to get rich from it and it all went wrong."

"And you personally killed him for it?" Ru insisted.

"No, I didn't! I swear."

Ru wriggled the knife around in Drews' leg causing him to scream and then cry. Ru had never seen a grown man cry like this before and a part of her felt sorry for him but only a small part.

"Please I beg you!" he whimpered.

"Is that what Mikey said before he died?"

Drew shook his head, tears of pain streaming down his cheeks.

"It wasn't my fault. I promise it wasn't my fault. They made me do it?"

"Who, who made you do it?" Ru shouted at Drew's face.

"The Wolves, they are behind all this. They used this drug on us, I don't know what really happened. I'm telling the truth! I couldn't resist them. Now please, take the knife out of my bloody leg," Drew whimpered pathetically like a beaten dog left out in the rain.

Ru pulled the knife out and a steady flow of blood began to seep from the wound. Suddenly the door opened and a young woman walked in. She saw Ru standing with a knife in her hand and a bloodied Drew strapped to the chair.

"Oh my God!" the new entrant screamed.

"Drew likes it rough!" Ru joked.

"I know but… this isn't right," the lady declared.

The young lady was beautiful and slim with straight blonde hair. She wasn't very tall but was wearing the biggest black heeled boots Ru had ever seen which meant she was slightly taller than Ru though most of the height seemed to be boot heels.

"This isn't right you idiot. Go get Sebastian or Reception. This woman is crazy," Drew ordered.

"No, stay here!" Ru barked.

The woman did a double take and stared at Ru, then Drew and then again at Ru before she scarpered. Ru couldn't risk her raising an alarm and she rushed across the room and caught the blonde before she got more than two steps towards the door, her mobility hugely impaired by her boots.

Ru grabbed a handful of her perfect blonde hair and wrenched her head back.

"Oww", she yelped.

Ru stretched her arm around the woman's neck.

"No, no, please don't hurt me" the woman screeched.

Ru tightened her grip and put her in a chokehold. Ru knew if the big guys couldn't resist then this poor little thing wouldn't have a hope.

"No, please. You can't do th..."

"Quiet!" Ru ordered.

The young woman fell silent within three or four seconds. Ru eased her grip slightly and walked her over to the bed, her legs able to just about walk without giving way.

"Now you just take a nap and keep quiet".

Ru tightened her hold and for a second the women reached up and pulled at Ru's hair but a second later her hand had fallen onto Ru's own hands that she tapped weakly.

"Noooo", she pleaded before she slumped forward until she was being entirely held up by Ru's grip on her neck.

Ru let go and the woman slowly fell onto the bed where she seemed to instinctively make herself comfortable as she fell asleep.

Ru looked down with satisfaction and then over to Drew.

"Now, where were we?" Ru asked as we walked back round to her tied up prisoner.

"Where can I find these Wolves? They've already attacked a friend and me."

"They are badasses man. People who mess with them end up dead. They're in West Watford, I don't know where. I try and avoid them. Look them up," advised Drew.

"You're going to spend a long time in jail if I have anything to do with it", Ru told him.

"It better be a long time because if I get out, I will find you and then I'll kill you."

Ru rolled her eyes.

"Whatever, Trevor."

She opened up her handbag and took out her phone. She hadn't expected to do so at the start of the evening but everything had worked out better than she could ever have expected and so she called Sgt Wilkinson.

"Hi, I can't say who I am but it's me. You gave me a card and said to call you if I have any information. Well, I have a whole police van full of information at the Penthouse Suite of The Grove so make sure you bring plenty of handcuffs".

In less than 10 minutes the doors opened and six police officers burst into the room.

"This crazy assed bitch tried to kill me!" he screamed at Sgt Wilkinson.

"I seriously doubt that," the sergeant replied.

"Look at my leg you idiot!"

"Untie him and take him away. We've been trying to get you a long time Drew." The police officer had a look of jubilation on his face as he spoke.

"His two friends are in the room next door and in the cleaners cupboard at the far end of the corridor, where ever Drew is going to, they should go too," Ru advised.

One of the PC's looked over at the stirring woman on the bed.

"What about her Sarge?"

Sgt Wilkinson glanced over at Ru.

"She's just a call-girl as far as I know. She's ok", Ru explained.

"Take her down the station, give her a caution unless you find out anything and then release her".

The PC nodded and with a colleague pulled the woman to her feet and carried her out of the room, her feet dragging behind her on the polished floor.

The Sergeant waited for the room to empty and when it was just him and Ru, he closed the doors.

"Miss, when I said to call me if you need anything, I didn't mean to call me to re-organise the duties for everyone back at the station. You've stepped well over the line".

"I know" Ru replied.

The sergeant sighed and put his heads in his hands.

"Look, we've been after this group for a long time. We didn't even know of all the guys at the bar that you messed up".

"These people, they killed Mikey", Ru explained.

"I know".

"So you believe me now?" Ru asked.

"It's not a question of believing Ru. It's a democracy, we can't just arrest people with no evidence. So that's why I'm glad you called me", explained the police sergeant.

"Glad?" Ru asked, her interest perked.

The officer nodded his head.

"We want you to work for us."

"As a cop, I mean police officer?" the rising tone of her voice indicated that her interest was well and truly piqued.

"No, no way. What I mean is, we're going to let you continue to sort through whatever it is you're going through but if anything goes wrong, we don't know you".

"You want me to do your dirty work?" asked Ru.

"You can do stuff that we can't, you can go to places, even our undercover guys would stand out a million miles. We have nice looking girls at the station but they are all known amongst the criminals and besides, none of them look like you or can fight like you either."

Ru was a little-taken aback, she genuinely never expected such an offer.

"What if I get hurt, or killed?" Ru asked.

"If you get hurt, we'd help as much as we can any other citizen. If anything worse happens then, we'll set Steve up with a new life and do our utmost to catch whoever did such a thing to you".

Ru smiled.

"It sounds a deal".

"Good. There are just a few provisos. There are some drugs involved in this case somewhere along the line. We want them." the police officer explained.

"Okay, if I find them then I'll bring them to you," Ru confirmed.

"You got to keep a low profile and don't go out of your way to kill anyone", the sergeant emphasised the last part of the sentence to make it clear to Ru where the limits were exactly.

"Not a problem, I don't want to kill anyone. I just want justice for my friend and to catch who nearly did Steve in".

"Do you need me to give any evidence?" Ru asked

"I don't want any evidence of you anywhere, at the moment. That young black kid Paul at the club, he blabbed most of what went on. I'm sure Drew isn't going to confess to any murder, we're hoping to get him on other things if the others talk."

"He murdered Mikey," Ru insisted.

"Well, you've got 28 days to get us the proof, to be sure that we aren't forced to release him".

The Sergeant walked over and examined Ru's cut arm.

"You should get that seen to".

"I will, Drew tried to kill me you know."

"Well when you get proof that he murdered Mikey, we can charge him with that as well.   You should leave here before I do".

"I understand," Ru nodded.

"Listen, thanks for your work. I know we can't help you that much but if you need anything, call me".

The police sergeant patted Ru on the shoulder for a job well done.

Ru flashed the officer a smile and walked out. V rules.

Chapter 12

It was approaching midnight by the time Ru parked up outside their home. For some reason, she looked around the street before she exited the car but there was no-one to be seen. The police had evidently found them the quietest street in the whole of the town.

Steve was still as she left him hours earlier on the sofa. He didn't know that she had done this to him and her sense of guilt had faded somewhat from the time of the actual events or maybe it had paled into insignificance compared to what had happened this evening. As soon as she saw him, though, she remembered that Steve was a big part of the reason she was doing all this and he didn't deserve to be treated this way. She figured that what she'd done to him was probably assault even if it was done in a loving way.

"I'm so sorry" she mouthed.

Realising that it wouldn't do his aches and pains much good if he spent the night like this, Ru went into his room, put the light on and pulled back the duvet.

"Come on sleepyhead, let's get you into bed," she said having returned to the sofa.

Steve didn't even open his eyes as Ru took most of his weight as she partly walked and partly dragged him to his bed, tucked him in and switched off the light.

She was still buzzing from the action this evening and made herself a hot chocolate which she drank as she looked on the internet for the cemetery where Drew had mentioned that The Walkers would be. Despite it being close by, it really was in the middle of nowhere. Her curiosity satisfied and finally feeling sleepy herself, she went to bed.

*   *   *

It was 9 am both there was even a sign of life in the house. Ru slept in just because she was exhausted, whilst Steve slept in as he didn't have much of a choice. After a showering and a very leisurely breakfast, the pair decided to have a very easy day.

Ru decided that they should treat themselves so they decided to go to Jimmy's World Food Grill in the High Street or the Met Quarter as it was nominally and pretentiously known in the town's planning department.

Both Ru and Steve loved Jimmy's, they served food from lots of different countries. Ru liked it for all the Indian food, a taste of home without the cooking. Steve loved it for everything, such a good selection of foods from so many countries that it was hard to not pig-out. By pig out Steve meant more than three stacked platefuls of food plus dessert.

Ru remembered the look on Steve's face the first time he saw how much she ate there. Apparently, the gym work meant she could eat almost whatever she wanted, so long as it was vegan.

It was between the second and third plate of food that Ru decided to tell Steve about Drew and her plans for The Walkers.

"I've got something to tell you Stevey boy".

"What's that sis?" He asked.

"Last night I err, I went to The Grove and one way or the other all the guys in The Bears have been arrested".

"What did you do, when did you go?" Steve demanded to know.

"Don't worry, I didn't do anything stupid. I found out that the guys who killed Mikey might not have been entirely responsible, they were made to do it by another group called The Wolves".

"They didn't hurt you did they? You shouldn't do things like this," Steve said both angered by her actions and worried about her safety at the same time.

"Actually, at one point I almost got killed, Drew smothered me with a pillow. It was bad man. Also, Mikey wasn't exactly innocent," Ru explained the adventures of her latest escapade.

Steve stretched out his hand and held Ru's arm, giving it a long squeeze.

"Did we ever think he was?" Steve asked, almost with a tone of hilarity in his voice.

"He was into gambling and drugs and he was playing off all these gangs. It got out of hand and they all wanted a piece of him," Ru explained.

"What about those guys who put the boot into me, so to speak?" Steve asked.

"The Walkers, yeah. I wanted to talk to you about them. How about you come with me on a stakeout? I want to take them down." Ru said.

"Actually, I don't want to go there but I'm going to because I know you'd go anyway," Steve replied.

Steve looked across at the food stations, it was almost empty around the lasagne, sweet and sour chicken and kofta kebabs dishes and he still had room for a third helping. Only in Jimmy's could such non-complimentary food go together so well on one plate.

"What did you do to The Bears?" Steve asked.

"I handed them over to the Police. Actually, that cop who came to our place a few weeks ago. We had a talk and we've come to a sort of understanding".

"Really? What kind of understanding?" Steve's curiosity piqued.

"They want to use me to clean up the place and get justice for Mikey, so long as I don't blatantly wreak a tornado of death and destruction across the place," Ru laughed.

"Be careful Ru. I bet they won't be of help if you get yourself in trouble. They might even lock you away for everything, it's not like what you're doing is entirely legal," Steve rightly noted.

"Not legal perhaps but it is right? Definitely." Ru replied.

"That's what I like about you," Steve grinned.

"I know", Ru smiled.

"So tomorrow we are going to do some detective work but for now, do you think we can sneak in a third plate of food before desserts?" Steve asked.

"Try and stop me!"

"Not a chance have I?" Steve asked.

Ru shook her head.

"Sorry bro, a girls got to do what a girls got to do!"

*   *   *

Having planned things out as best as they could over dessert, the next morning they set off at 10 am in Ru's Audi. They had some rope and wires in the boot and both had spent quite some time looking at the cemetery on Google Maps beforehand.   There was only one road to the entrance and the cemetery was in the middle of nowhere, formerly a burial place of patients at the Victorian Leavesden Asylum including possible Jack The Ripper.

It took about 20 minutes in the car to get there. The cemetery itself was now disused and overgrown and the one-track lane petered out into a muddy ditch a few hundred yards up the road so it was certainly quiet.

They parked well out of sight of the cemetery confident that no-one else would be driving this way. Steve was dressed in combats and a parka coat whilst Ru had for once not felt like dressing up at all. Her first choice of jeans with slits in the knees she decided not to wear, not because of the cold but in case she had to crawl around on all fours so she had settled for leggings and a hoodie. She thought she wouldn't stand out from the crowd if there were any crowd to stand out from.

"So what's the plan?" asked Steve.

"Well there is only three or four of them so I'm going to take them out one by one" Ru explained.as she got some items out of the car boot and put them in her pocket.

"What about me? Don't make me be the Xander", Steve said in reference to the wise-cracking but physically useless in a fight friend from Buffy The Vampire Slayer.

"You go round the back and make sure no-one escapes. If you see I need help then come on in but only if I need help. I'm the professional here!" Ru teased.

"Whatever, Buffy!" Steve retorted.

Ru waited as Steve walked down the lane to the side of the cemetery. It was enormous and entirely overgrown with only one or two footpaths still free from weeds. Ru hid in some bushes near the entrance to the cemetery which was marked by a beautiful though also creepy looking wooden archway. She knew from her research that there was an old concrete bunker of some description at the far end of the graveyard and that was likely the place where the group was holding up in but she hoped to avoid charging in there with all guns blazing, especially as she didn't have any guns.

After about 15 minutes Ru was beginning to get a sore bum when a young man strode in under the archway. He was in a hurry and wearing a hoodie with his hood up but he wasn't looking over his shoulder at all, so was seemingly not expecting anyone to be around.

Once the man was 10 feet or so in front of her, Ru sneaked out onto the pavement. She had found and old shovel in the undergrowth and brought it with her knowing she could give it a new lease of life.

Ru looked around but she couldn't see anyone else. The man was marginally taller than her and it was hard to see his size due to his baggy clothing but she guessed he was kind of average though he was walking quicker than many jogged. Ru felt strangely exhilarated to be out in the open and about to take down a seemingly helpless chav like a lion toying with the isolated gazelle.

She was just a few feet behind him now when all of a sudden the man stopped in his tracks and knelt down to tie his shoe laces. Ru was forced to stop too lest he somehow heard her footsteps through his hoodie, A few seconds later the man stood up and started walking but at a slower pace. Ru hurried to catch him, the man paused. Had he heard Ru? She wasn't sure but she was now just inches behind him.

Not wanting to kill him she did her best to plan what was coming and she raised her shovel above her head before bringing it down upon his and at the last minute before contact, slowing up. She hoped it would knock him out but not fracture his skull especially as he was wearing a thick hoodie. There was a dull thud and silently the man fell to the floor, just managing to raise his hands to protect his face before he became motionless.

Ru stopped and took a deep breath. There was no-one else that she could see so she bent over and checked the gangster was basically unharmed. Fortunately, he had only just landed next to a broken stone cross. Ru was sure it was as much down to luck as to her skill as she tied his arms up before dragging him into the undergrowth.

Ru circled round and went into a dense thicket of laurels and hid there for what seemed to be some time just listening to the birds and the rustle of the trees when she saw movement on the path into the cemetery. A strong looking fair haired man was walking up towards the bunker. He was dressed all in black except for some white trainers and he looked considerably smarter and more capable than the hoodie wearer.

Ru watched him disappear inside the hideout only to reemerge a few minutes later with a drink. He took a sip and placed it on the roof of the old concrete bunker. It was then that Ru decided to make her move. She picked up a large heavy tree branch and as quietly as she could, walked up behind him. At the last minute she spotted a large lump of rock so finding the branch a little cumbersome, she swapped it for the boulder and moved into position.

The man didn't even know what hit him as Ru brought the rock down upon him. However he was too tall to hit properly on his head and the rock too heavy to lift to such a height and so Ru hit him on the base of his neck. It was still enough to send him reeling to the floor. Dazed he was still able to move and so Ru brought the rock down onto him twice more. With him sprawled helplessly on the ground, one final blow sent his nervous system into overload as his arms twitched before he fell silent.

Ru was delighted, such a change from the night before. She has these guys wrapped around her little finger, so far no-one had even seen her, let alone offered any resistance, her belief and the opinion of Drew that The Walkers were small time crooks seemed to be bearing out. It was a big relief that she hadn't got herself into a fight. She tied the man's hands behind his back and lugged him into the darkest and furthers corner of the bunker. It wasn't exactly cosy but there was a paraffin heater inside, along with a table and a few chairs.   Bizarrely there was a sofa on the roof of the old ruin, quite why even criminals would want to catch some rays in a Victorian cemetery was beyond Ru.

She had thought to stay inside the bunker to see if anyone else arrived but she didn't like the idea of being hemmed in and so she went outside and lay down in some long grass, well away from the bunker and pavement.   Though the damp ground made her uncomfortable, it was more the fact that she was laying amongst gravestones that made her skin crawl most of all. She hoped the residents wouldn't mind too much. If Mikey were here, Ru thought he'd probably comment on them getting a good view of her boobs or bum.

Half an hour of hiding later and a third gang member entered the fray. He was wearing jeans and a dark sweatshirt. He looked a bit messed up, obviously spending a few days in the cemetery had taken its toll on him. Ru thought that perhaps he was looking for his colleagues as after taking a cursory look inside the bunker, he went the length and breadth of the cemetery.

Ru was thankful that he hadn't found anyone and when he decided to sit down on a bench it was then that she decided to go in for the kill.   As she walked round behind him, she noticed that he pulled his phone out and made a call.

"Excellent, use up one of your arms why don't you," she smiled.

Ru stopped and took out a bottle of drugs which she had prepared putting on a glove in case she spilled any on her skin she poured a small amount onto a cloth and gave it a quick sniff. It didn't really have a smell though she could feel its effects on her eyes and so pulled her head away quickly.

She hadn't tested it before but seeing as she was a pharmacist and had degrees in biology she thought that it should do the trick. Hopefully, it would be a lot quicker than the tablets she had relied on in the past plus it had the advantage that she didn't have to risk getting into a fight or, at least, she wouldn't if she got a good grip on her prey.

Quietly but purposefully, Ru walked right up behind the seated individual. His call either hadn't lasted long or he hadn't managed to get through, maybe because the recipient was laying face down in the mud Ru thought to herself. Instead, he was writing out a text message when to his complete surprise, Ru smothered his face with a chloroform laced cloth in her hand.

The man immediately dropped his phone and tried to shout, being taken entirely by surprise. Ru wasn't sure how long the drugs would take to work and she was taken aback when the man managed to stand up almost impervious to what was going on and temporarily escaped from her grip. However, she soon realised that it was a temporary setback and it must be working as he as he swayed slightly.

"That's as far as you're going Mister" Ru ordered as she smothered his face once more and grabbed hold of his shoulder.

For a second Ru thought he might escape again but then she seemed to gain control and pushed the man back down onto the bench. She had big hands and the one with the cloth covered his face almost from ear to ear. The man tried to pull her hand away with both of his but he could barely get a grip and when he did he wasn't strong enough and instead she pulled his hair, forcing his head right back where was able to take an even better hold.

"You're going to take a nice long sleep aren't you", she purred.

Soon one of his arms started thrashing around and trying to grab anything it could. Ru took hold of his hand and held it still as his other repeatedly but ever more feebly tugged at the one held over his face before it went still while holding onto Ru's. His breathing went shallow and his body limp as Ru felt him fall back into her arms. Even as he lay almost horizontal, she kept the cloth pinned to his mouth and nose and all the man could do was take in breaths and fall ever deeper under her control.

At last, Ru let the man go. He looked like he didn't have a care in the world, boy was he in for a shock when he awoke. Ru decided that she'd wait another 15 minutes after tying this man up but no-one else came on the scene. As she waited, she checked the man's phone. It had all sorts of contacts on it which she thought might prove useful one day so she entered details into her own phone.

There was a noise in the bushes behind Ru and she instinctively swung round. She took a sigh of relief when she saw it was Steve.

"Wow Ru, I'm glad you're on my side".

"Yeah, don't mess with V" Ru joked which made Steve laugh.

"Can you call that Sergeant Wilkinson and have him send a police van to Leavesden Country Park and meet him there".

"What about you?" Steve asked.

"I'm going to put this lot in the car and drive them around to the park. They'll never get a big van up this lane."

"Ok, do you want a hand?" Steve asked.

"No, it's ok. Just get over to the park. I can handle sleeping beauty here. It's when three of them wake up that there might be problems."

Nevertheless, Steve helped Ru carry the hoodie guy back to the car, he was the heaviest and it was he who had hurt Steve the most in the flat when all of this started. He was glad that they had caught them and though happy that they would soon be going to jail, just a bit of him wished he could hurt them as much as they had hurt him.

They dumped him in the boot of the car and left his legs sticking straight out as Steve went off to call the police and have them meet Ru in the car park of the nearby recreation ground. Ru went back to retrieve the more smartly dressed criminal who had come to in the bunker. Ru had to threaten him with another beating before he came with her. When he saw that Ru intended to bundle him into the car he tried to escape.

Ru thought it was funny as he couldn't hope to get very far with his arms tied behind his back but he was shouting and determined not to go quietly. Ru took out her cloth again and brought it to his face but as he saw it approaching he held his breath and so it had little effect.

"I'm not standing here all day" Ru complained before kneeing the man relatively lightly in the groin. He didn't fall over but it did make him start breathing again and he soon crumpled to the floor and as he fell Ru directed him into the boot.

The final gang member was still laying on the bench and Ru did her best to carry him back to the car. The boot now being full, she thought about putting the final man in the back seat as she had planned but something made her think that after all they had done to Steve, they all deserved to be in there together and so she threw him on top of the others.

Though there was no way for them to escape, she didn't want them to damage her car so she gave each of them a quick sniff of her potion whether they wanted it or not and closed the lid.

While Ru wasn't sure that she liked her work, she knew that V loved hers and she fired up her Audi, turned the stereo up loud and put the pedal to the metal. The engine revved and the wheels span sending clumps of dirt flying into the air. She was happy that she had caught the gang that had beaten Steve to within an inch of his life and was determined that he be around to see them taken into custody.

When she arrived at the park just a few minutes later, Steve was sat on a tree stump next to Sergeant Wilkinson and another unfamiliar police officer. She pulled up her car next to the police van.

"I think you've been looking for these," she said.

Ru opened the door and pulled the three groggy individuals out of the boot and plonked them on the tarmac.

"This is what you get for messing with my friends", she shouted down at them.

"You are being arrested for Grievous Bodily Harm, illegal entry of private property and 16 counts of money laundering and gambling activities. You do not have to say anything, but it may harm your defence if you do not mention when questioned something which you later rely on in court. Anything you do say may be given in evidence." said the sergeant.

"Ok, put them inside," the sergeant said to his colleague.

"Thanks, guys. And remember, we were never here" the sergeant said as he helped load the van up with the three men, none of whom were protesting in the slightest.

"Come on Steve, let's go home," Ru said.

The windows down, the music up, Ru soon had the car roaring through the narrow lanes back towards home.

Chapter 13

The next few days went by relatively calmly. Steve was happy to continue his rest and recovery while Ru was still trying to think about how to tackle The Wolves and hopefully tie together all the loose ends. Ru knew that she had been lucky against Drew and perhaps more than a little casual about the whole thing yet her operation against the gang in the cemetery had reminded herself that she was more than capable of beating almost anyone if given the opportunity. That being said, it seemed likely that The Wolves would be the most daunting opponents of all and it was very likely that they were in some way aware of the one woman crusade that was out to get them.

She had spent extra sessions at the gym to work out her aggression whilst also going to her private sword fighting club. Ru had always admired ninja's and samurai not just for their physical prowess but also their whole way of life. Probably though it also came down to that swords were just incredibly cool and she had a set of three that practiced with.

Such was the case today; not really having made much progress as to where to find The Wolves and yet incredible slightly missing going to work, Ru wanted to feel the buzz of combat without actually fighting anyone.

Meanwhile, Steve was at his computer as he been for much of the last few days, he had been building a dossier on The Wolves. As much as he could tell, it was headed by two twins, Wakim and Aisha with the rest of the crew made up of an extended family. They were into drugs big-time and ran a number of restaurants as well as a strip club which Steve guessed was mostly just a front, maybe as a way to launder their drug money.

He'd had some success though this morning, he'd used some special computer software and after finding an online photo of Wakim, managed to trace the picture to one on his Facebook page. It seemed he went spent most of his time at the gym near The Country Club, this would be what Ru needed to work her in and so Steve printed out all the information she would need to find him.

Steve felt guilty that Ru had put it upon herself to get justice for Mikey and even for himself. Frustrated with things, Steve decided to check out a hunch and maybe even be a little bit useful. He got dressed, well more dressed than he had done for the last few days and got in his car. It felt strange being in the driving seat, he hadn't driven since before the attack but as soon as the engine came to life he felt more at ease.

He decided to drive to one of the Indian restaurants associated with The Wolves and kill two birds with one stone. Firstly get some food and surprise Ru and secondly see if he could validate or obtain any information. He knew that Ru would metaphorically kill him if she found out what he was doing but sometimes sitting at the computer researching, being the back-up wasn't good enough. Besides, by all accounts The Wolves were by far the baddest gang in town and if he could sort things out and save Ru the danger then why shouldn't he?

It was a 15-minute drive to The Bangalore, it was located just off St. Albans Road and not in an area that he often visited. He parked on one of the countless rows of terrace streets and grabbed his phone. He switched on the voice memo app and pressed the record button before dropping it in his jacket pocket.

"Just in case," he said to himself.

The sign on the restaurant said open but there didn't appear to be any customers inside. Steve opened the door and was greeted by a tall and slim waiter dressed in a smart black waistcoat and dark purple shirt.

"Eat in or Takeaway Sir?"

"Takeaway, please. Can I have a Chicken Balti with Bombay Aloo, plain rice and a Keema Naan." Steve nearly always had the same Indian food wherever he went. He wasn't into the namby-pamby mild curries and could eat the hottest available or indeed the hottest jalapenos on pizza come to that but there was just something right about a chicken balti.

"All the Balti dishes come with rice", the waiter chipped in

"Oh, great. Can I also have a vegan curry with rice and a plain naan."

"Certainly Sir. Do you want any poppadoms with that?"

Steve nodded his head.

"Especially if you do Mango Sauce," Steve enthused.

"If you'd just like to take a seat and your food will be ready in about 15 minutes," the waiter explained with a smile before walking off.

Steve sat down on the end most seat on the row of chairs and waited. He wanted to do something but what could he do? Twice he opened his mouth to say something but promptly closed it when nothing came out.

"Excuse me, Wakim isn't here is he?", Steve said feigning familiarity.

"Sorry sir, he runs our other restaurant", the waiter replied rather tartly.

"Does that mean Aisha is here?" Steve asked again.

"What do you want with Aisha?" the waiter asked, his tone of voice suddenly sterner.

"Nothing, well. I'd like to talk to her about Mikey and the stuff he owes her".

"Are you police?" the waiter asked, his eyes glowering at Steve with suspicion.

"Who me, no way" Steve replied.

Steve watched as the waiter picked up a phone.

"Aisha", was pretty much all Steve could deduce from the conversation as it was conducted in an entirely foreign language which brought out a sigh of despondency from Steve.

The waiter put down the phone and a few seconds later another waiter appeared.

"Do you want to come with me for a few minutes whilst chef gets your order ready. Aisha doesn't like to do her washing in public."

Steve thought twice about agreeing to the request but didn't see too much harm in going as he was only going to tell the truth. He hadn't done anything himself so why would anyone want to do anything to him except hearing what he had to say? Steve was led through the restaurant, past the kitchen to a store-room that doubled as an office round the side. The walls were covered in shelving housing bags of rice and spices of all persuasions whilst at the back wall sat a small computer desk with a young woman sat at work. Hearing their footsteps, she stopped what she was doing and sound round in her chair.

"I'm Aisha, what can I help you with?"

"Tusi kaisai ho?" Steve said remembering one of the politer phrases that he had heard Ru greet some of her Indian family.

Aisha stood up and Steve was immediately taken aback by how stunning she looked given that Wakim didn't look all that, at least in his Facebook photo. She was tall and slender, dressed in a suit with long black hair in a ponytail, mauve lipstick and beautiful blue eyes which Steve guessed must have been due to some sort of contact lenses.

"You speak our language?" Aisha smiled and extended her hand for Steve to shake. As Steve shook her soft hands, he noticed that Aisha gave a nod which seemed to be the signal for the waiter to leave them as Steve could hear him walk off back towards the door.

"My name's Steve. Listen, I don't know quite how to say this but I'm a friend of Mikey. I know that Mikey was double-dealing with you and that other gang but you shouldn't have killed him".

"We didn't kill him, I know people used to think restaurants used to use cats and dogs in curries but never humans". Aisha replied, sitting back in her chair.

"That was a joke by the way!" she laughed.

Steve let out a nervous laugh "Nice one!"

"Why are you here? I mean really?" Aisha asked.

"Now I'm here, I'm not sure why I came… My friend, she's a bit of a badass and she has already worked her way through The Walkers and The Bears. She's set her sights on you now as she got a confession out of Drew".

Aisha let out a sigh.

"Anyway, sooner or later she's going to get you unless the police come first of course. I just wanted to tell you and give you the chance to hand yourself in, I don't want anyone else to get hurt. Especially my friend," Steve said, suddenly wondering if he was talking himself into a body-bag.

"I've heard about your friend. Vixen isn't it? Well, thanks for the tip-off but no-one important is going to get hurt, well not myself in any case. Does anyone know you're here?" asked Aisha.

"No, no-one. I just played a hunch. I can leave and never come back, well not unless the Balti is nice…. That's a joke too," said Steve.

"I'm really sorry about your friend but it has nothing to do with us. Now, if you will excuse me, I have work to do. By the way, you spoke Punjabi earlier, we're Pakistani, we speak Urdu".

Steve was disappointed, was he even entirely wrong about the whole situation? He couldn't be; otherwise he wouldn't have been invited round to the office. Either way, he hadn't got very much information and most likely he would be tailed so that the gang could find out where he lived. Aisha hadn't admitted anything about Mikey but then she wasn't likely to come clean about a murder in her own backyard. Interesting that she was in some way familiar with Vixen. That wasn't a crime of course but surely she must be involved somehow as even the police hadn't publicised V in any way.

Steve nodded his head, turned and made for the door. He'd taken just a few steps when he heard Aisha open an office drawer. Something made him turn round to see what was happening. Through the corner of his eye saw Aisha pull out a gun though not like any gun he'd seen on the television before. Instinctively he ran for the door and was halfway there when he heard a bang and then his body was overcome by the most mind-numbing and incapacitating pain. Mid-stride, he fell to the floor face first, his arms and legs writhing from the 50 thousand volts running through his body.

"I am sorry Steve, you seem a nice guy and because you're a nice guy I just shot you with my Taser rather than a gun," Aisha said looking down at him.

"I wasn't joking about the curry, though. Mo, tie him up and take him back to my place. I would have killed you and Vixen, in any case, you've just given me the chance to to find out what I need to know first so I appreciate that. Once we've had a friendly chat, then I'm going to kill you Steve and your friend Vixen too," said Aisha assuredly.

Steve didn't have time to utter a single word of defence or defiance as seconds after pulling out the prongs from the Taser, Aisha walked round and kicked him hard in the face with her boot.

* * *

Steve awoke to find himself in a dark and unlit room. Steve wasn't sure where he was or how much time had passed since he as with Aisha, what he did know however was that his hands were tied behind his back and seemingly secured to some sort of pipe. He couldn't move his legs either so it seemed likely that they had been bound together as well. Steve didn't need a mirror to tell that he had one hell of a black eye from where he'd been kicked in the face. Another one to add to the collection of bruises, cuts and fractures he mused.

Steve lay there cold and uncomfortable for an indeterminate length of time. He was sat on a cold hard surface but he couldn't quite make out what it was. His thoughts kept drifting to Ru, she would be worried sick about him if only she even had an inkling of what had happened.

However Steve was unsure whether he had been unconscious for 10 minutes or 10 hours and aside from leaving details about Wakim, he had left no information as to where he had gone. It was likely that he would be a goner long before the cavalry showed up.

Just then the door opened, the light flickered on and Aisha accompanied by big, burly man entered. Steve could immediately see that he was being held in a bathroom, a large luxurious bathroom but a bathroom none the less which meant it likely he was in a private residence rather than in the back of a restaurant somewhere.

"Say 'Hello' to Steve, Mo", Aisha smiled.

"Hello, Steve", Mo said gruffly.

"You'll have to excuse Mo. Conversation isn't his strongest suit. You remember how bloodied up Mikey was when you found him. Well poor Mo here, gets frustrated with people when they don't answer questions," Aisha explained.

"I had a feeling he wasn't here for his good looks," Steve said wryly.

"Now tell me about the drugs Mikey had, where are they?" Aisha asked.

Steve shook his head.

"I'm sorry but I don't know anything about them."

Mo bent over and punched Steve to the right of his face. Not being able to move or put his arms up, he was a sitting duck and there was nothing he could do to prevent the crushing pain that came down upon him so hard that his head bounced back against the wall. It took Steve almost a minute before he could talk again.

"I don't know anything about the drugs, I just know Mikey was up to his neck in them. I never saw them, I promise!" Steve insisted.

Aisha waited a while for Steve to compose himself, she bent down and grabbed his cheeks with her thumb and forefinger, squeezing them together.

"Listen you Tattee Choad, who is your friend? Where does she live?"

Her eyes were just inches from his and though there was beauty aplenty in them, he could find no kindness or compassion.

Steve shook his head which brought a slap from Aisha to which he responded by spitting in her face. This brought on the possibly the biggest and strongest ever kick that Steve had ever received in his life. Mo barged past Aisha and booted him so firmly in the stomach that the force pulled the radiator pipe that Steve had been secured to away from the wall. Not that Steve noticed as he was winded so badly, he couldn't breathe and he rolled around on the floor in total agony.

"Don't be like Mikey. I'm going to kill you anyway but it can all be over very quickly", Aisha pleaded.

"Tell me what her name is?" Aisha screamed.

"Her name is V. V is for Vixen".

Steve was in such agony and so severely dazed that for some reason, he started laughing, quietly at first and then almost uncontrollably.

"What the hell is so funny" demanded Aisha.

"I'm just thinking about how she is going to totally and indisputably kick your ass and then she's going to kill you," Steve confessed.

Aisha motioned her head towards Steve and Mo stormed forward and punched him twice in the stomach and then once in the face. As an unintended final act of defiance, Steve slumped motionless at Mo's feet.

"We're not going to find out where she lives today. Wait until he wakes up, knock him about again and then leave him and lock the door."

"Don't worry cuz, I've got it all taken care of", Mo growled.

Chapter 14

Ru pulled her car into the driveway.

"That's weird".

She noticed instantly that Steve's car had gone. It hadn't been moved for ages and, in fact, was used so infrequently that there was moss growing along the rubber lining at the base of the windows.

As unexpected as this was, Ru didn't stop to question it for too long. She had already worked off her frustrations for the day with an energetic if undemanding session with her sword and she presumed that as Steve was now much better, he had just gone out for a drive and catch up on some of his errands.

She went inside their house and had a shower before even noticing the note that Steve had left for her on the sofa. There was a photo of Wakim, possibly the joint leader of The Wolves gang and a brief message:

'Apparently he hangs out at the gym next to The Country Club, thought you'd like to check him out. He's the top dog! Good luck Ru :-) '

Ru felt a tinge of excitement well up inside her.

"Thanks, Stevey-boy!"

Quickly, she poured herself a glass of soya milk and then went to get changed into her backup pair of gym clothes and decided to follow the lead that Steve had left her there and then. Grabbing her keys and her now ubiquitous bag of goodies, she headed back to the car where she found it still warm inside from only 20 minutes ago.

It didn't take long to get to the gym and the car park was mostly empty except for a few new Audis, Jags and the odd company car BMW. It was in quite an exclusive location and it came as little surprise that if Wakim was loaded from his drug acquired dosh, then this would be exactly the sort of place Ru expected a poser like him to hang out at.

At least, Ru presumed he was a poser going by his photo. Tall and athletic rather than well-built and with a close-cut haircut and an overly white smile that would stand out in the snow. Ru thought he definitely loved himself and Vixen was finding out that those sort of guys were amongst the easiest to ensnare.

Ru decided to park her Audi next to a maroon coloured Jaguar, the gravel surface crunching under the wheels of her car. She walked round to the entrance of the beautiful old Edwardian house which must have belonged to the neighbouring Country Club in a previous life and rushed up the stone steps, through the pillars and into the Reception area where an attractive blonde young lady was sat behind the desk.

"Hi there, I'm here to see Wakim... is he around?" Ru blagged.

"Are you a member?" she woman asked without looking up from her keyboard.

"No, but he said it would be ok for me to go on through so he could show me the ropes as his guest". Ru spoke so convincingly that she, at least, convinced herself that she was speaking the truth if no-one else.

The lady looked up at Ru and Ru tried not to let the thought that she the woman appeared to be a bimbo to show through on her face.

"Ok, through the main doors. I'm sure he will be on the running mills, that's where he normally is," the receptionist explained.

"Thank-you!"

With a spring in her step, Ru went through the pair of heavy wooden doors. It may be an expensive gym but in the end, it was just a gym with areas devoted to exercise bikes, rowing machines, weights and cross-trainers. There was a line of eight treadmills at the far end of the room and that was where Ru headed to.

There were only five other people in the gym and Ru guessed that Wakim was the only one running on the treadmill. He was wearing black shorts and a matching top and sported a chunky gold chain around his neck that belonged in Fort Knox. He was running steadily on the machine second from the left and though Ru could have started running on the most distant machine to the right she decided to pick the neighbouring treadmill to her nemesis. She wasn't here to get fit after all but to get his attention.

The controls of the treadmill were almost identical to the ones in her own gym so she removed her jacket and pulled down her fleece pants so she was just in her shorts and top, set the speed limit and started running. For exactly five minutes she didn't even glance to her left, she just concentrated on running as steadily as she could while looking as relaxed and fit as possible. After five minutes passed she stole a glance to her left and saw Wakim watching her before she once more looked ahead and ran for further five minutes.

She had barely worked up a sweat when she looked at Wakim once more and seeing him staring at her she let on a coy smile before returning to attention to concentrating on her running. Ru was reasonably confident she could keep this pace up for an hour but didn't think she would have to wait that long for Wakim to try and worm his way into her affections and this was confirmed when a minute later he stopped running and wiped himself down with a towel. Ru continued running but could feel his eyes on her so she was almost grateful when he broke the ice and spoke up.

"You're pretty fit... you Indian or Pakistani?" He asked.

Ru stopped running and did her best to answer without sounding out of breath.

"Brummie", she replied.

It was clear from the puzzled look on his face that Wakim didn't catch her drift.

"Brummie, you know… Birmingham," Ru tried not to let her disgust at him show through.

"Yeah, I get you but where's your family from?" He asked.

"India", said Ru.

"Aww, you're still pretty fit, though. I'm from Karachi", Wakim sounded a little disappointed before almost immediately perking up.

"You fancy going out for a bite to eat?" Wakim asked, trying not to come over too sleazy.

"I don't normally go out to eat with strange guys I've just met but as you like running, why not!. Do you mind if we go in my car?" She responded.

"No man, that's good innit".

Ru stepped off the machine and put her jacket on. It suddenly came to her that Wakim was one of the men who broke through the windows that night when she and Steve were watching TV in the flat. Obviously in the dark and commotion, he hadn't got a good look at her.

"I'm Wakim by the way."

"V" smiled Ru.

There may have been only four other guys working out in the gym but she was pretty sure that all four of them turned their heads as she walked the length of the hall and out of the door.

As the pair entered the carpark, Ru clicked on her key fob and the indicator lights on her Audi blinked.

"Nice set of wheels you have here V," Wakim complimented her.

Ru had barely driven out of the carpark before it became evident that Wakim had intentions other than lunch at The Holly Bush pub when he put his hand on her thigh and made a comment that Ru found repulsive, at least coming from him. Still she did her best to hide her true feelings. V was a professional business woman and her business was taking down the scum.

Half a mile further down the lane was a grass bank overshadowed by a broadleaf woodland. Ru knew that traffic very rarely passed this way in any case and a smile came across Ru's face as a vague plan entered her mind. Wakim obviously misread the smile for something entirely different when Ru parked up.

Wakim moved forward to kiss her but Ru shook her head.

"No, not here!" She said before opening the car door.

"I much prefer the outdoors, just look at the woods and it's so private in there. Believe me, I know", Ru winked cheekily.

Ru stood by her door and waited as Wakim got out the car and walked around the car to meet her. Ru put her arms around his neck and gave him a gentle kiss on the lips before appearing to accidentally drop her car keys.

"I'll get them for you", Wakim said.

Ru watched as Wakim bent over and measured him up. As he was bending back up, Ru grabbed his hand and kneed him in the groin which had him curled up in an instant.

"Thanks for that!" she exclaimed gleefully as Wakim angrily shouted abuse at Ru and tried to grab hold of her.

Ru wasn't going to have any of it and she jumped back in her car, started the car and pressed the button down for the car window to come down. As expected, Wakim staggered towards the window and screamed at her.

"What the hell are you doing?" Wakim shouted furiously.

Ru reached out and pulled his gold chain around the steering wheel, put the car in first gear and started to drive.

"You crazy bitch, I'm going to kill you," he shouted.

At first, Ru only moved at walking pace until she was sure she was off the grass bank and back onto the road.

"Your days of killing people are over bruv" Ru answered back before she began to slowly increased the speed.

His chain entangled around the steering wheel forced Wakim to walk alongside Ru and his face was just inches away from hers.

"You are dead" he yelled as he reached over and put one hand around Ru's neck and the other went onto the chain, trying to untie it from the wheel.

Ru tried to remain calm, she didn't let the small fact that Wakim was very badly trying to strangle her change her tactics. Of course at any time, Ru could put her foot on the accelerator and literally rip his head off. If that wasn't her fist choice, she was still very much in control of the situation, it's just that Wakim didn't know it yet.

Ru put her foot down on the accelerator only slightly harder and the speed increased incrementally forcing Wakim to begin jogging to keep up otherwise he would strangle on his own necklace. Unexpectedly, somehow Wakim managed to free himself from his chain with the result that he managed to strengthen his hold on Ru's neck with the other flapping around trying to

Alarmed, Ru grabbed hold of his flailing hand and increased the speed.

"Stop, stop, I'm telling you!"

"If you have enough energy to yell, you're obviously not running fast enough," Ru laughed.

Ru went faster now and after 10 seconds she felt the hold around her neck lessen and then his hand let go all together which immediately tried to pull her hand off his one but to no avail and he was soon compelled to release his grip.

Ru knew she had him where she wanted now and held his hand in hers with a vice like grip digging her nails into his skin. As the speed increased, Wakim stopped splurging defiance at her and instead had to do his utmost to keep up.

"You like running, let's see how far you can keep this up. I've got 405 miles left showing in my tank, how about you?" Ru smirked.

They were going at 12 miles an hour now and Ru could see the strain etched on Wakim's face. Ru blew him a kiss just because she could and she hoped it would aggravate him. Watching carefully, she saw after a few more seconds that Wakim was tiring and it corresponded with her no longer feeling him resisting her in any way. In fact, now almost the only thing that was keeping him on two feet was the fact that Ru was towing him along through their hands.

After 0.6 of a mile Ru slowed down from a fast sprint pace to more of a jog but by now that was that she needed to do and besides her arm was tiring now from pulling his weight along so he had little doubt he was as good as finished. She slowed the car down to 5 miles an hour before pressing down on the breaks suddenly forcing Wakim to come to a sudden halt, his shoulder hitting against the door frame.

Ru noticed that there was blood coming seeping out between her fingertips, she knew the blood wasn't hers.

She let Wakim go and he immediately slumped to the floor panting heavily.

"Stand and deliver bitch, your money or your life!", she shrieked as she climbed out of the car.

Wakim looked up and with great effort swung his fist up towards Ru's face but he didn't come close to making a connection as Ru simply took a step back. Wakim fell forward onto all fours and did his best to stand up straight before Ru punched him twice in his stomach and as he stooped over, kneed him hard in the face.

Wakim fell to the ground, he wasn't unconscious but he nearly was and Ru watched as he tried to pull himself up by gripping onto the car wing mirror. She bided her time for almost a minute until he lifted his head up straight at which point Ru was ready and she punched him venomously in the face. She had plenty more where that came from but it wasn't needed and after initially not seeming to have an effect, Wakim's eyes rolled back and he slumped back against the car before finishing in a heap against the car tyre.

Ru went and opened up the boot and removed the cable ties and rope, placing them temporarily on the car roof.

"Here, let me help you with that," Ru said as she dragged a groggy Wakim round to the boot of the car.

"And I thought you were going to give me a bit of a workout. There's you as sweaty as a pig and here's me just ready to play."

Ru stood him steady against the back of her car, but he slumped over, she was just messing around of course but she'd always wanted to do this like in the movies. She pulled Wakim up and leaned him more heavily against the car before taking a step back and putting all her weight on her left foot and sprang out with a kick from her right. Her shoe made a perfect connection with the chin of Wakim and he went flying backwards into the boot. Ru wasted no time securing his arms behind his back, her work was done, she slammed the boot door closed with a thud.

Ru found that she had worked up an appetite and so went off to The Holly Bush pub in any case. It was a smart old coach house, almost in the middle of nowhere but still busy with lunchtime revellers with people taking a break from their workplaces. Ru parked at the furthest spot in the car park away from the pub and ordered an Apple Tango and salad.

Despite the barman being more interested in how long it took for Ru to get such a firm stomach, she finally managed to get away from the bar and go and wash the blood that covered her fingers. Who'd have thought her manicure would have a practical use? She felt a real buzz as she knew that Wakim was one of two people who started this whole chain of events off, discounting Mikey himself of course.

Returning to her table, she got her phone out and tried calling Steve but there was no answer. Ru thought it was was out of character and so sent him a text to see if he was ok, hopefully, he would get in touch soon.

Ru was hungry and devoured her meal, it was hard being a Vegan in any case but even harder when eating out and, to be honest, she never found salads very appetising but she was polite to the barman and told him how much she enjoyed it when she walked back to her car.

Ru decided to open the boot door, for some reason, she was paranoid that Wakim had escaped even though that would seem impossible what with the door being locked and the back seats being immovable from inside the boot, she knew this as she had tried it herself. The door lifted open and Wakim was still unconscious, lying exactly where he had fallen half an hour earlier. She closed the door and got back in her car.

Theoretically, she could take Wakim to the police but they might ruin everything and stop her enjoying herself. There'd be a time and place to involve the police again but the time was not now. Instead, she knew exactly where she was going to take him and she doubted anyone would ever think of looking there.

Chapter 15

There was no-one around in Stonefield Close when Ru parked her car outside of the abandoned warehouse. All the cars from the neighbouring dilapidated buildings had gone for the day and only the distant hum of traffic gave any indication that there was any life around at all.

Ru had tried to telephone Steve several times but each time the call had gone to voicemail without anyone picking up. Similarly half a dozen text messages had been delivered but not read; that's if the status reports could be believed. Steve never liked using the phone but she knew he would, at least, respond to her even if my messenger pigeon. She was getting worried and time was running out. The stakes had been raised and Ru felt it was time to Call or Raise.

Exiting the car with some rope in her hand, she climbed through the hole in the steel fencing that she had been through two times thus far before poking her head through the wall which she was also intimately familiar with. She was being cautious just in case there was anyone around but she knew, of course, that there would be no-one as she had already defeated every one of the gang members who had been here and involved in the death of her friend.

Cold rays of sunshine shone through the small row of windows that passed through the small section of offices at the far end of the empty warehouse as the sun began to sink beneath the horizon. After making absolutely sure that she was alone here, Ru went back outside and opened up the car boot where Wakim still lay exactly where she had left him. She bent over and hauled him out of the car. Carrying a man wasn't like carrying a gym weight and she found him hard to get a good hold off as she plonked him feet first on the roadside.

"Come one wakey-wakey," she said, slapping him twice about his face.

It didn't do much good and though he stirred, his legs crumpled like a pack of cards forcing Ru almost to drag him to the fence before pushing him through the hole limb by limb. Once squeezed into the warehouse itself, Wakim became more aware of his surroundings. However being aware of his predicament and being able to do something about it were two entirely different things and despite some token verbal insults and feeble resistance, he was frogmarched to the middle of the warehouse where he soon found his wrists tied together in the centre of the warehouse floor.

In the middle of the floor was a big heavy hook which Ru could see to be fastened to a grimy industrial chain. The links to the chain were about an inch thick and they ran up sixty feet to the ceiling above where they attached to a large overhead industrial crane. Ru took her length of rope and secured his arms to the hook with a tight knot.

"Right loverboy. You're not leaving this place until you tell me who exactly killed Mikey, where I can find your sister and what has happened to my mate Steve. I don't care in which order but I advise you to get talking".

Vixen had put on her meanest and toughest talking badass persona yet and it wasn't all an act. The way Ru was feeling now, she could very much do something drastic and she didn't think she would regret it either.

Ru walked the short distance to the crane's control panel which hung from the ceiling on a long rubber hose. It was dark and oily and not the sort of thing Ru particularly wanted to touch but things were going to get a lot darker for Wakim if she had anything to do with it.

"I don't know what you're talking sis." Wakim stammered.

"Look, there's been some misunderstanding. Untie me and we can sort you out with something to make you happy," he continued.

"Don't 'Sis' me!" Ru scolded.

"I've never worked in a factory before but these controls look easy enough. Buttons for up and down....side to side and a green to start and a red to stop I guess".

Ru pressed the green button on the crane controls. She listened hard but couldn't hear if anything happened or not as Wakim stared at her bemused.

"Let's try the 'up' button shall we?"

As soon as Ru pressed down on the button with her thumb, the hydraulics in the crane came to life with a low hum. It didn't take long for the chain to tighten in the air before link by link, the chain on the floor was hoisted into the air.

Ru watched as Wakim looked, at first, her and then the feet of chain on the factory floor as it tightened up.

"Are you crazy?" he yelled.

Ru smiled back.

"Definitely a bit crazy," Ru nodded gleefully in confirmation.

"You can't do this to me," Wakim shouted.

"Good luck with that, you piece of shit", Ru grinned. "It says's here that the crane can handle loads of 20 tonnes which is probably even enough to deal with your ego."

Ru quite enjoyed watching the chain uncoil from the floor and wondered what would happen when there was no longer any slack left. She didn't have long to wait as it pulled at Wakim's arms. He took two small steps forwards towards the chain before his arms were hoisted above his head. A few seconds more and his feet lifted off the ground.

"Wow, I bet even your mother wouldn't say you were an Angel?" Ru giggled.

She watched as Wakim was pulled higher and higher, shouting for help but there was no-one who could hear him.

"It's just you and me Wakim, just as you wanted it at the gym I bet. If you shut up for a minute, I might press stop".

Wakim complied and Ru pressed the red button on the control panel. The crane fell motionless and Wakim swung gently forty feet above her head.

"Are you going to talk?" Ru spoke asked gently? "Or do you want me to ram you into the ceiling?"

"You can't make me do anything. You need me", a flustered Wakim insisted.

"Where is Steve? Where can I find your sister? Who killed Mikey?" Ru asked.

"Don't know what you're talking about babe," answered Wakim.

"Fine, have it your way".

Ru turned to leave and began walking back towards the exit.

"Just remember, the crane might handle 20 tonnes but I doubt the cable ties will last long with you. Maybe a few hours, maybe you'll be lucky and have lost consciousness before they snap. If you're lucky, perhaps you'll just be permanently disabled from the fall rather than turn into in a Wakim pancake".

The warehouse was silent except for the echo of Ru's footsteps reverberating around the empty shell of the warehouse walls. Just as she disappeared behind the racking, she heard Wakim shouting.

"Come back, I'll talk. Just come back!"

Ru swivelled around on her heels, victorious she returned to her helpless prey.

She pressed the 'down' button on the controls of the crane and watched as effortlessly the chain lengthened sending Wakim back earthwards. She reached up and extended her right arm and just before his feet were back on the on terra firma, Ru stretched her hand around Wakim's throat before pressing stop on the controls.

"Talk", said Ru, her thumb and fingers tight around his neck.

"I don't know anything about Steve. We've been looking for you, not him".

"Why has he disappeared today then?" Ru asked.

"I don't know!" Wake said, his eyes bulging and his head shifting around uneasily in Ru's grip.

"Seriously, I was at the gym… you came to me remember. If Steve were around before you left him, I couldn't have nothing to do with it innit".

Ru rolled her eyes, what he said was actually plausible but she was totally convinced he had been taken and that Wakim or his sister were at the bottom of it.

"Where can I find your sister. Tell me and you have my word I won't kill either of you".

Wakim shook his head.

"Tell me now or I'm going to choke the life out of you!"

Ru squeezed harder with one hand while simultaneously punch Wakim in the groin with the other. She hit him so hard that his neck escaped from her grasp and he went swing back on the chain writhing in agony as he did so.

"Bloody well tell me, you stinking piece of shit!" she screamed so loudly that Wakim closed his eyes, genuinely terrified at his helpless predicament.

Ru didn't wait for Wakim's pain to subside and punched him again but in the stomach before reaching for the crane controls and sending him 20 feet into the air.

"Unlike you, I'm not going to hang around all day," Ru informed her prisoner.

Seething, Ru marched towards the makeshift exit in the wall, the moans of Wakim falling into the distance. She had hoped it wouldn't come to this but she had brought them along for a reason. She returned to the car and opened the back passenger door, taking out the long slender black case that lay under the seat.

Quickly, she hurried back into the building and put the case on a rack of shelving. She opened the casing, inside were three Samurai swords and without a moment's hesitation, she removed the longest one from the case.

As she strode cockily back towards Wakim, she unsheathed the weapon and let the end of the long blade drag along the concrete floor sending sparks flashing through the air. Ru could tell before she even reached Wakim that she had his total attention.

"I don't know about you but I read this cool book called '101 Most Horrible Tortures in History'. I always loved tortures; they're sick I know but they're also fun aren't they? At least, if you're the torturer!"

"You're a sick mofo, woman." Wakim writhed in mid-air trying with no success to free himself from his industrial restraints.

Ru pulled the tip of the sword up and having quickly prodded Wakim in the ribs with it finally settled on pushing the blade up against his neck.

"There was that one where they would break something every day. It would all start off very mundane and inconsequential before escalating into something very deadly. Maybe they'd start off with a hair or a nail, then a fingertip, then a hand to an arm... a leg but that would take a long time".

"You are dead!" Wakim screamed.

"You know what, you're right. I am so terrified of being threatened by a guy I've already beaten up, now have suspended by a chain in an abandoned warehouse while holding a sword that I am going to let you go", Ru shrugged her shoulders meekly.

"Seriously?" Wakim asked.

"Shit no! Only one of us is going to be dead in a minute and it ain't the hot girl and highly trained girl with a sword."

Ru started walking round Wakim, circling him and watching his unease each time she disappeared behind his back.

"I've always liked that one 'Death by 1,000 cuts. The idea behind it is quite simple, rather than quickly killing someone with one or two blows the victims instead endures hundreds and hundreds of minor wounds… well, minor-ish…. if they were on their own but together they have to hurt".

"Who killed Mikey?" Ru demanded.

"You wouldn't dare", Wakim shook his head defiantly.

Ru lowered the sword and pushed it into Wakim's shirt before thrusting forward, creating a large rip through the material before she pulled the sword down and created a tear all the way down to his waist. A second jab with the blade created another one and soon his entire chest and stomach was exposed.

Now that Ru could actually see his flesh she took a step back and stretched our her arm fully so the blade rested on his flesh. Quickly she swiped it down creating a narrow, bright red flash running up and down the right side of his stomach. Wakim screamed and instinctively tried to pull away but hanging from the crane as he was; there was nowhere to go, nothing to hide behind.

Again Ru stretched out and slashed him on the left side of his stomach.

"I'm gonna be playing notes and crosses on you before we're through"!

"Stop it. Stop it! Who the hell do you think you are?" Wakim pleaded.

"My name is V and don't you forget it".

Ru swung her sword repeatedly, this time making incisions on his thighs and then his chest.

"That's got to smart a bit, let me have a look at that?" Ru mocked as pretended to inspect one of his stomach wounds.

Wakim screamed out loud as she raked his wound with her nails.

"I can keep this up all night. To tell you the truth, I'm just getting started but you can stop it all now. Tell me what I need to know."

Tears were streaming down Wakim's face, Ru wasn't sure if he was crying from fear or just in agony. Hopefully both, she thought to herself as she walked behind Wakim and started systematically sweeping his back with her sword and a small puddle of blood began to form on the grey concrete floor.

"Stoooop! Please, I'll tell you everything. Please, I beg you. Just stop. You've won alright!", Wakim begged before sobbing his eyes out.

"Don't ever underestimate me and have no doubt I'll carry on if you don't tell me what I want to know" Ru instructed.

"You can find Aisha on at "118 Woodland View off the Croxley Road. It's the white house with the columns by the front door, the one behind the conifers. If she has got Steve then sooner or later, he will end up there".

"And what about Mikey?" Ru asked

"What about him…. It wasn't me okay. Maybe it was Mo or Aisha. Please, just let me go".

"I can't do that; you might be telling me anything. I'll come back and get you tomorrow once this is all over".

"There could be 5 or 6 people in there. When Aisha sees you, both you and Steve are screwed!"

"For your sake, you better hope I make it then".

Catching Wakim totally by surprise, she planted a punch right on his chin and he fell silent.

"Nice work V", Ru said to herself.

Ru tore a bit of Wakim's bloodied shirt and fastened it round his mouth as a gag, tying it behind he heads before she raised him back towards the high warehouse ceiling.

Her work here done, Ru hurried back to the car. It was nearly dusk and there was a distinct autumnal chill in the air as she put the headlights on before turning the key and roaring the engine to life.

"Let's go finish the job".

Chapter 16

Ru had tried calling and texting Steve again throughout her drive home but she was getting nowhere. It was a forlorn hope that he might be sat at home innocently watching television with his phone on silent down the back of the sofa but she didn't really believe that would be the case.

As soon as their house came into sight, she could see that Steve's car wasn't in its usual spot. Something was very wrong and her mind raced through a number of increasingly negative possibilities and grizzly conclusions. She would never forgive herself if Steve were to suffer a similar fate as to Mikey.

Once inside it was clear to Ru that no-one had been there since she had closed the front door at lunch time. The kitchen remained untouched, the cushions on the sofa still lay as they had at breakfast time and a quick look inside Steve's bedroom revealed the bed remained freshly made.

Ru toyed with the idea of calling the police but it was far too late for that now. She was in it deep over her head and if the police got involved now, it would likely alert Aisha to what was happening. Not to mention get Ru in all sorts of trouble. No, it was clear that she could only rely on herself and aside from a little help from Steve, that is what she had done all along.

Ru went into her bedroom and got changed into something altogether more black and V-like. Then she went to Steve's computer desk and had a rifle through the drawers until she found what she wanted, an envelope. She grabbed it and hurried into her bedroom. Bending down, she reached under the bed and pulled out a large cardboard box. Inside was the large consignment of Devils Breath, which was held in a large transparent re-sealable plastic bag. Ru had hidden here as she knew Steve would never chance upon it in her room.

She carefully opened it up and using the envelope as a trowel, Ru scooped as much as she could of the potent drug inside before tucking the lid of the envelope inside so as to close but not seal it.

There didn't seem much point in hanging around even though she was determined not to rush into anything and after stopping to have a glass of water and verifying the address information that Wakim had given her on Steve's computer, she headed out of the door. There wasn't the time to make a plan, she knew what had to be done. One way or the other she knew that she had to do what she always did, put the bad guys out of commission.

It was dark outside and spotting with rain which encouraged Ru to sprint the short distance to her car. Jumping in, she placed her stash of drugs on the passenger seat underneath her swords. The last thing she wanted was that flying all over the place.

She knew where the street was that Aisha was based in but wasn't overly familiar with it and especially not of the house. The traffic through Watford was awful, Ru thought it likely due to Christmas shoppers clogging up the roads and it took her over 40 minutes to make the relatively short journey across town. She hoped to hell that she didn't get pulled over by for a minor traffic violation. Getting caught with weapons and drugs by anyone out of Sgt Wilkinson's team was likely to be a one-way trip to jail.

Ru drove the length of the street to scout out the area. As it transpired, the house was exactly where Wakim said it would be and she parked her car a few hundred metres down the road. Ru picked out a long dagger from the choice of three bladed weapons she had with her and put the other two under the passenger seat.

Getting out of the car she tucked the dagger in its scabbard between her belt and her jeans on her right-hand side so that it didn't get in the way but was quickly available if needed. She folded the envelope in half and put it in the inside pocket of her dark burgundy hoodie that she was wearing. Her outside pockets had several cable ties in case she took any prisoners and so she thought she had something to cover every eventuality she could reasonably expect to encounter.

There seemed little point in locking her car though she did of course. The street was lined with plush houses with cars that made her Audi look like a battered old Fiat. Besides something told her that no-one would do much crime so close to the headquarters of the Wolves Gang.

When she reached the house, it was hard to see very much at all. The boundary of the property was lined with thick conifer trees behind a 6-foot tall brick wall while the driveway was gated off behind sturdy looking oak gates. After double checking that there was no-one on the street to see her, Ru jumped halfway up the wall and used her arms to pull herself up onto the top of the wall and into the dense green foliage of the trees.

There didn't seem to be any people or dogs in the garden but she took the time to examine the place as best as she could in the dark. It was a large house, Ru estimated it could have six or more bedrooms as well the obligatory Games Rooms and Saunas that houses in this part of town always seemed to have. For a moment, she toyed with just ringing on the front door and fighting her way in as if she were in some sort of Quentin Tarantino film. As excited as that might be, Ru thought it a certainty that there would be CCTV around the doorway and having a stranger at the front door, with the gate well and truly closed would only get things off on the wrong foot.

To the left of the house but not quite adjoining it was a double garage block. It was separated from the house itself by the width of a footpath but parallel to it was a partially open window on the first floor of the house. She decided that this would be her route inside.

Ru lowered herself as far as she could down towards the ground before dropping the last foot or so. Quickly she scurried across the lawn to the garage block and shimmied up the drainpipe until she could haul herself up onto the flat roof of the garage.

Ru was anxious not to make a sound in case the open window alerted the inhabitants to her whereabouts but fortunately, the patter of the now increasingly steady rainfall muffled the noise of her movements to those inside.

From her vantage point, it was easy to see that the lights were on inside the room and the sound of some dance music was audible though not particularly loud. She knew that someone would be in the room if music were playing and as the open window was only partially open, she wasn't able to leap directly onto the window sill without hitting the window first. Therefore, her only option was to jump over onto the window, somehow open it and scramble inside before being noticed or attacked.

Ru felt her breathing increase and she could feel her heart pounding loudly as she took a short run-up and launched herself across the chasm and landed on the outside of the window, her hands grabbing hold of the top of the window with some difficulty due to the rain making it slippery. She knew she only had seconds and reached inside to the window handle and unlock it, let alone losing her grip and falling to the ground below.

Reaching in with her arm, she grabbed hold of the window handle and yanked it desperately in every direction until it finally moved. Instantly the window swung wide open sending Ru against the external wall of the house before she managed to manoeuvre herself to the narrow edge of the window and then swing the window back towards the closed position before jumping inside.

No sooner had her feet touched the ground when she realised that she was inside a gym room all fully furnished with exercise bikes, rowing machines, treadmills and weights amongst other things. To her alarm, there wasn't just one but two people inside. Both young Asian men in their twenties or thirties. The one at the far end of the room was pedalling away on an exercise bike and hadn't yet noticed anything was amiss but Ru found herself already under attack from an energetic individual who was running over towards her with a dumbbell in his right hand.

He swung it hard at Ru's head but, fortunately, she ducked in time and it collided into the wall with a dull thud which had the effect of immediately sending the man off-balance. Ru lost no time to go on the offensive and grabbing his head, rammed it twice into the wall. The man dropped the heavy dumbbell to the floor and Ru was about to punch him when she noticed the second individual sprinting across the room to confront her. Seizing her moment, she took two small steps forward and then pounced feet first with a flying kick, connecting with her attacker broadly on his chest sending him flying backwards.

Quickly she jumped to her feet to find the first gym fanatic about to strike her but she blocked his punch before jabbing him with two of her own. With a few seconds to evaluate the situation she grabbed the dumbbell and chucked it across the room at the second man who was only now finding his footing and though it missed its target, it had the effect of making him lose his balance and Ru watched as he fell backwards onto the floor again. Ru only hoped the noise wouldn't bring up re-enforcements as she already had her hands full.

The ten seconds of respite this bought her were all that she needed as Ru laid into the man reeling at her feet with a headbutt which sent him reeling back against the wall before he crouched down on one knee.

"Perfect" Ru squealed as she stretched out a leg and kicked her assailant full in the face. She smiled as she realised he was out cold before he even fell face first to the floor.

"Who are you? What are you doing here" the sole survivor shouted across at her as he set about uncoupling the weights from adjacent weights bar.

However, he was far too slow and had only succeeded in removing one before Ru was virtually on top of him. His plan foiled, he instead thrust the weight towards Ru's stomach with such desperation that it sent Ru flying back to the floor. Though Ru wasn't even winded, she lay writhing on the ground, hoping to feign injury and so lure her victim in. Just as Ru had hoped, when he approached she kicked out with both feet at his right leg sending him crashing to the floor.

She hovered over him waiting for him to get to his feet which he was very slow to do so, in the end, Ru grabbed his head and pulled him up.

"Come and fight me like a man!"

She grabbed his neck and pushed him back against a wall. She didn't have to push hard as he was instinctively cowering away from her.

"Tell me, where is Steve? Where can I find Aisha?" Ru demanded to know.

There was no reply. Instead, the man just shook his head.

"You're pathetic," she said as she reached into her pocket and took out the envelope.

"You see this, this is Devils Breath. You guys killed Mikey for it and one way or the other you're going to tell me what I want to know".

With one hand still on the mans neck, she used the other to carefully open the envelope and then she let him go when she had to use her hand to retrieve some of the powder but then the man tried to punch her forcing Ru to slam her body against his and into the wall.

Then took a pinch of the powder in her hand and blew it into his face. She waited a few seconds and repeated her question.

"Tell me, where is Steve being held?"

Instead of profusely offering an answer, the man just smiled at her.

"You clever mother, you just held your breath because you knew what was coming. Well, let's see you handle this" Ru shouted angrily.

She punched the man in his stomach with all her might which sent him doubled up with an agonising groan. Ru hurriedly poured out another small dose of the drug and raised her palm right under his nose. He grabbed her arm for support but in his winded state he had no option but to breathe the powder in and Ru immediately felt his aggression subside.

"Feeling a little bit less tetchy are we?" Ru asked.

The man didn't reply and nor did he resist when Ru stood him back against the wall as a blank expression fell upon his face.

"Good. Now tell me, where can I find Steve?"

"He's in the second bathroom", the man whispered.

"How do I get there from here?" She asked.

"Go out the door, turn right. Go to round the corner and it's at the far end of the landing".

"Is Aisha there?"

"Yes", the man replied in his now enforced monotonous manner.

"How many others are there in the house?" Ru questioned.

"Just us two, Aisha and Mohammed".

"Where is Mohammed?" Ru asked.

"I think he is in with Steve, they are going to kill him this evening, if it hasn't happened already", her assailant spoke calmly, entirely helpless to answer every question that Ru put to him.

"Does anyone here have any weapons?" she asked.

The man nodded his head.

"Aisha has a pistol but she doesn't normally have it in the house".

"Well done! Now, I'm going to give you this cable tie. I want you to take it and go and tie one wrist around that exercise bike and then go to sleep. Do you understand?"

"Yes", the man nodded his head, took the cable-tie between his thumb and fingers and walked off. Ru had such faith in the drug that she didn't even watch him and instead went over to the other individual who lay heaped in a ball.

She dragged him over to the weights bar and tied both of his hands to the steel pole. There was no way in the world he would be able to move from the angle which she had left him in. Her work in the gym almost complete, she dried herself down with a towel before walking over to the window and shutting it tight. Turning round, she saw the other gang member securing himself to the pole under the bike saddle before slumping to the floor.

"Wow, that is good stuff," Ru mused.

She waited for a moment until everything was silent and then went over to the door pausing for just a moment to switch off the lights. There was just one last thing to do now, the only question was whether she could do it. Opening the door, she peeked her head round the corner and seeing that it was all clear she left the gym and closed the door behind her, confident that neither of the occupants would ever trouble her again.

The landing was tastefully decorated with bare oak flooring and white-washed walls. However, it meant that Ru found her footsteps to echo round the interior so she slowed to a crawl and proceeded almost on her toes to ensure the maximum stealth. Sure enough, she reached the bend in the corridor and turning left she could see the stairs to the ground floor, a number of bedrooms and a door at the end of the landing.

Anxious she peered over the bannisters to see if there was anyone below, the lights were on but there wasn't even a hint of life down there and so she picked up her pace and hurried over to the end of the corridor. The door was shut but she could hear voices from the inside. It sounded like a man and a woman, she couldn't be sure but Ru thought it to be a safe assumption that it was Aisha and Mohammed. She listened intently for nearly a minute and though she could hear them shouting at Steve, she couldn't him reply. She hoped he was okay, at least, he was alive.

Ru took a deep breath, realising that she didn't really have a game-plan once inside the room. All that she could really hope for would be that she would be able to muddle through the situation somehow. At least, she had the element of surprise and she intended to use it. Ru put her hand on the door handle and held it still for a moment before pulling it down and swinging it open as hard as she could.

In one giant leap, Ru sprung into the room and between the force from her and the door, Aisha was sent splattered against the wall. Ru could see Steve well and truly alive though terribly bruised and bloodied about the head and torso and looking entirely vacant. He looked beaten to within an inch of his life and if that actually scared Ru, it also caused her to become even more combative than she already was.

Mohammed was leaning over Steve, yelling into his face and was caught totally by surprise by Ru's dramatic entry. By the time he had turned round, Ru had already launched into the air and kicked him square in the face sending him crashing into a white washbasin which collapsed under his weight, smashing into a dozen pieces on the floor right next to where Steve lay.

Ru turned round and ran over to Aisha and attempted to put a sleeper hold on her but before she got it locked on effectively, Aisha bit her deeply in her arm, forcing her to relinquish her hold. Instead, she walloped Aisha twice on her back and kicked her to the floor before returning to Mohammed. He lashed out with his fists, missing with one but striking home with the other. However, Ru felt impervious to the blow and grabbed his head and twice slammed it into the white ceramic tiled wall.

Seeing Aisha still struggling on the floor, Ru decided to do her best to finish off Mohammed and threw him into the bath. Quickly she clambered in behind him and she pulled down the metallic shower hosing, hit him about the face with the shower head before wrapping the hosing around his neck and pulled it as hard as she could.

Mohammed tried to grab Ru's sword and succeeded in pulling it out from under her belt but when she saw the danger she kneed him in the face. The sword fell with a clatter on the side of the bath before hitting the floor next to Steve.

Ru pulled the shower hose tighter, she felt like she could pull it so hard it might snap his head off and she yelled with weeks of pent up anger and frustration. Ru didn't see Muhammed turn a deep shade of purple but noticed that he went limp several seconds before she let him fall face first into the bath.

She was about to climb out when she heard Aisha scream.

"Stop or I'll shoot!" Aisha shouted.

Ru turned to see Aisha standing just a few feet away, a pistol held very firmly in both hands and well out of Ru's range to kick or punch it away.

"You bitch! You think you can just march into my home and think you can get away with it? Get out of the bath and stand in the corner," Aisha ordered.

Aisha waved her gun left, motioning for Ru to stand in the opposite corner of the bathroom from herself. Gingerly, Ru climbed out, avoiding Steve's legs and the broken radiator and washbasin as best as she could.

"Alright?" Ru asked.

Steve blinked his eyes and gently nodded his head.

"You might as well put the gun down, the police will be here soon. Turn yourself in", Ru explained earnestly even if she knew that nothing could be further from the truth. No-one knew they were here and who would emerge the victor would be entirely down to Aisha.

"Really?" Aisha asked.

"Cos I don't think so. In fact, I have friends in the police if you know what I mean," she continued.

"Yeah, well we will see how many friends you have after I get you to confess to murdering Mikey… as well as all of this", Ru tilted her head in Steve's direction.

"You know, I'm letting you talk shit because you, your friend here are both going to be dead when Mohammed wakes up. You'll end up in the same landfill as that idiot Mikey. That's what happens when you mess with The Wolves. This is my house and I make the rules".

"Dream on you tart" Ru replied.

"Now unless you want me to kill Steve here very slowly and painfully, you're going to tell me exactly where the drugs are that Mikey has and the stash of money that he appropriated too."

Ru shrugged her shoulders.

"Don't know anything about the money and if I did, I wouldn't tell you!"

"Then I don't have any use for you", Aisha smiled.

As both of the women had been trading verbal blows, neither of them had noticed that Steve had reached out and slowly extended his arm and taken hold of Ru's sword. Though he had absolutely no energy left, seeing that Ru was about to be shot, somehow he mustered everything he had to lunge at Aisha, sword albeit sheathed in hand.

Steve was slow having been beaten to pulp and confined to the floor for most of the day but his actions still caught Aisha entirely by surprise and instinctively she turned towards Steve and pulled back on the trigger. There was a deafening crack as the noise of a firing gun reverberated in the small tiled bathroom. Ru watched in horror as just two steps from Aisha, a point blank range Steve got hit.

Three thoughts ran through Ru's head almost simultaneously. The first obviously the total horror of seeing Steve shot and hoping against hope that he would survive. The second that he would fall straight down and not require another bullet.

Whether her first thought would prove to be the case, Ru didn't know but in mid stride, he fell to the ground motionless. Ru screamed. Steve had sacrificed himself for her and she wasn't going to let his bravery go to waste and so she decided to enact on her third thought, which was to overpower Aisha while she was momentarily distracted.

Ru rushed towards her and as Aisha levelled the gun in Ru's direction, Ru kicked it out of her hand, sending a bullet flying harmlessly into the ceiling and the gun to the floor. Aisha swung a punch at Ru and it connected well, stopping Ru in her tracks. As Aisha stepped forward towards her, Ru somehow managed to compose herself and shoulder barged Aisha in the stomach and the pair went crashing into the bathroom door which flew off its hinges and toppled backwards out onto the landing.

Ru found herself laying on top of Aisha, who in turn lay flat on her back and winded on the door in the landing. Aisha reached up and pulled Ru towards her by the hair only to punch her twice in the face which made Ru scream in pain. However rather than fall back Ru slumped forward and just when Aisha tried to scratch her face, Ru took hold of her hands. Aisha wasn't very strong and Ru managed to push them back to the floor before leaning forward and unexpectedly striking Aisha with a head-butt.

In truth, it probably shocked Aisha more than physically hurt her but it allowed Ru to take control and while her opponent was dazed she reached into her pocket and took out the envelope of drugs.

"You wanted to know where your drugs are. You're going to find out right now".

As Ru opened up the flap of the envelope, Aisha reached up and put her hands around Ru's neck squeezing it tight. She knew that she only had a few seconds but rather than try and release the hold instead continued to take a pinch of powder out and put it in the palm of her hand and with the last gasp of air in her lungs, exhaled and blew the powder down onto Aisha. Instantaneously Ru saw Aisha's eyes cloud over and the look of determination on her face melt away. The iron stranglehold around her neck lessened until Aisha might have been gently clutching a delicate flower stem that she didn't want to break. Ru slapped the hands away effortlessly and let out a deep breath.

"Steve!" she shouted as she crawled on the floor over to her friend. He was conscious but barely and breathing very fast. She took his hand and squeezed it tightly.

"You're going to be ok you hear me," Ru cried.

With her other hand, she fidgeted for her phone in the back pocket of her jeans. Pulling it out she tapped in 999.

"Hello, yes I need the police and ambulance right away to 118 Woodland View. Someone's been shot," Ru said, trying her best to remain calm enough to be understood by the telephone operator.

"Steve, Steve. Why the hell did you jump into the gun like that? You didn't have to do that for me".

Ru knew that Steve would have done the same thing for anyone just because that is the type of man he is but she had a feeling that's not the only reason why he did it for Ru and the immensity of it all overwhelmed her. For the first time since the whole series of events had unfolded she found her eyes welling up and tears began to stream down her face. No-one had ever shown her such kindness before. This could change her entire life.

"You better not die, Steve. If you do, I will bloody well find you and kill you".

Ru thought she saw Steve respond.

"Was that a hint of a smile?" she asked him.

It was then that she realised she had the opportunity to get the evidence from Aisha before the police arrived and when she would then be given the chance to speak to solicitors and deny everything.

She momentarily left Steve and crawled back over to Aisha, who lay calmly on the floor of the landing. Ru switched on the camera on her phone and went to video mode before selecting the recording button.

"Aisha can you hear me?" Ru asked.

Aisha replied that she could.

"Who killed Mikey?"

"Mohammed killed him," Aisha confessed.

"Where did he kill him Aisha?"

"At an old warehouse in Stonefield Way. He used Devils Breath to make the other gang help him and dispose of the body".

"Is that Drew?" Ru continued.

"Yes," Aisha replied.

"Why did Mohammed kill Mikey Aisha?"

Aisha didn't reply, it was as if she was trying to fight the drugs she had inhaled.

Ru stroked her head.

"It's ok, you can tell me" Ru purred hoping to remove any last inhibitions that Aisha had about confessing.

"I ordered it to happen. Mikey had our drugs and the money."

"And did you and Mohammed do this to Steve?"

Aisha nodded her head before Ru turned round and quickly video Steve on the bathroom floor.

"And you shot him didn't you?" Ru asked, turning her attention back to Aisha.

"Yes, we were going to kill him anyway".

"You stay here you understand, you're not to move until the police arrive okay?"

"Okay", Aisha confirmed.

Ru left Aisha and quickly videoed the bathroom of destruction before focusing the image on Steve after which she stopped recording. Mohammed was still laying face down in the bath so she returned to her friend and held his hand between both of hers.

"We did it, Steve. We did it for Mikey. You and me! I just want to say I'm sorry about all this, maybe we should have just left it to the police. Also thanks…. I came here to save your life not for you to save mine."

Steve's eyes were closed and a small pool of blood lay near his waist.

"Oh God no, you can't die Steve. I need you!" Ru was in tears, her mind and body exhausted and shocked.

Suddenly there was a loud bang from downstairs, followed by a second. Ru knew it was the police ramming the front door down and, sure enough, seconds later she could hear shouts downstairs.

"Up here, quickly!" Ru shouted.

What sounded like a herd of Elephants rumbled up the stairs. It was the police closely followed by an ambulance crew.

"Please, help him. This woman here shot him, he's been held prisoner here".

"Stand aside Miss. What's his name?"

"Steve," Ru said as she backed away into the corner of the bathroom.

"Jesus, what happened here?"

Ru turned to see Sgt John Wilkinson along with an increasing number of other police.

"There are two more in the gym at the other end of the landing", Ru said.

The Sergeant nodded and four constables headed back down the landing,

"I've got a full confession from her. On Mikey, this… everything" Ru explained, waving her phone in the face of the police officer.

"I'd like to see that one day", the sergeant smiled.

"I thought you might", replied Ru.

"Bloody hell Ru, you've gone way beyond what I expected".

"You mean I'm in trouble".

The police officer shook his head in admiration.

"No, I mean bloody hell Ru… you've done a super job. You've single handily brought down a string of gangs that we haven't been able to lay a finger on physically or legally. Well done. I'm sure there are going to be legal complications but I can assure you that we will do everything we can to make sure that everyone is made to pay for the crimes committed.

"Is he going to be okay?" Ru asked the ambulance crew.

"We don't know yet. He's in a bad way as you can see. We've got get him to the hospital right away if he's going to have a chance".

"Sarge, her brother, Wakim… he is at the old abandoned factory or warehouse in Stonefield Way. I had to rough him up a bit to find this place as I knew Steve didn't have long".

"No problem, I'll send some people to bring him back", Wilkinson replied.

"You might want to oversee that personally if you get the picture".

"I get you", the sergeant nodded.

"Can I come back in the Ambulance with you?" Ru asked, stretching over to pat Steve's hand".

"Are you family?" one of the first-aiders asked.

Ru nodded her head.

"Sort of".

"You might want to get your arm seen too" Sgt Wilkison commented.

"I will but not yet. Not until I know…" her sentence tailed off.

Ru watched as the ambulance crew transferred Steve onto a stretcher and carried him out of the room.

"I'll be in touch" Ru shouted over her shoulder as she followed Steve down the stairways.

It was then that the police officer heard in the noise, he bent his head over the bath and saw Mohammed stirring.

"Shit", the young Sergeant said both taken by surprise and taken further aback by what the scenes of total destruction that Ru had left in her wake.

"You're nicked son".

Chapter 17

A small crowd of mourners gathered together in a huddle as flurries of snow blew across the cemetery. Though there weren't any tears, there were sniffles as the coffin was lowered down into the grave. The mourners were mostly a rough, hagged mix of people but they were all his friends. Ru closed her eyes, all she could think of was her unfortunate friend.

"We, therefore, commit his body to the ground; earth to earth, ashes to ashes, dust to dust; in the sure and certain hope of the Resurrection to eternal life." said the old white haired Vicar, who had no doubt, said them thousands of times during his long life.

"I'm sorry Miss", Sgt Wilkinson leaned over and whispered in her ear.

Ru nodded her head and reached out to Steve, who had stood all the while the remains of Mikey were lowered into the Earth. The pair held each other close. The events and actions they'd lived through had brought them a unique understanding and connection between the two of them in a way few others could understand. Not needing to talk, they stood hand in hand in silence thinking of the sacrifices made. Finally having lasted as long as possible, Ru helped Steve sit down back in his wheelchair.

It had been 3 weeks since that night when Ru had brought things to a close and Steve had been taken into emergency surgery. Luckily the bullet had missed the vital organs and after four hours in the operating theatre, the surgeons had managed to stall the internal bleeding. It would take time though for him to recover not just from the gunshot but the numerous broken bones. One doctor had even commented he had seen more working bones in a jellyfish.

Faced with overwhelming evidence every single person who Ru had confronted, were either already in jail or facing a hefty prison sentence. It was during the plea-bargaining that young Paul, the very first gangster who Ru had dealt with all that time ago in the club had told the police where Mikey has been buried. Four days later his remains were found in the landfill and now he was here, laid to rest with some dignity.

With the service over, the crowd began to melt away. The police sergeant offered to help push Steve along the stony path back towards the carpark.

"What's the plan, Miss?

Ru shook her head, she did have a plan but wasn't sure if now was the time to tell the police officer.

"I'm not certain yet. I'm no longer working at the pharmacy though I've been offered a position as a Locum. I'm not sure that's what I want to do with my life, after all, this".

"You could always join The Force".

"What as a Jedi or a WPC?" Ru joked.

"Either way, we'd find a place for you," he said.

"Hope you get back on your feet soon Steve. You did a great job too, I'm sure Ru is very proud".

"She would have done the same for me," Steve chipped right in.

"But at what price... you lost your house, your friend, you've been beaten to within an inch of your life at least twice and you got shot."

"If I had done nothing, the price would have been my friend and my soul," explained Steve.

"Well, whatever happens, I hope it all works out for you both. Remember you've got 4 months to be walking again."

"4 months. Why 4 months, what's happening then?" Ru and Steve asked, almost in unison.

"Oh did I forget to tell you? Maybe I did in all the chaos. Well, you've both been nominated for community and bravery awards. In a few days, you should be getting a letter from The Palace with the formal notification of when you will receive your medal".

"Seriously? Nominated by whom?" Ru asked.

"Yeah, you better not be pulling my leg because that would be agony and it would probably come off in your hand", Steve joked.

"No, for real. I nominated you and was backed at the highest of levels".

"No way!" Ru shrieked.

"Listen before you go, I've got something in the boot of the car for you Sergeant".

Ru pressed her key fob and her car indicators bleeped before she opened up the back of the car. Inside was a large box, it was the Devil's Breath.

"You had this all along?" the Sergeant asked.

Ru smiled meekly.

"Sorry, it's all there well apart from a few grains". Ru explained.

"Well, at least, we have it now. Our boys looked all over the place for it in your old flat, Mikey's flat and car and all the places associated with the gangs. We even checked the salt and sugar bags in the stores of that Indian restaurant".

"We found it in the boot of Steve's car when we moved out from the flat," Ru explained.

Steve looked up in total amazement.

"We did? I don't remember anything about that" he asked.

"Yeah... actually I've been meaning to tell you about that. Remind me when we get home".

"Did you ever find the money?" Steve asked.

The sergeant shrugged his shoulders as best as he could considering he was carrying a heavy box of drugs.

"No. Did you?", the Sergeant replied to Ru, who frowned.

"I wish. Well someone, somewhere is going to have a very nice surprise one day", she laughed.

"Let's hope it goes to someone who deserves it, maybe even someone who will do some good with it." the police officer opined.

Ru and Steve watched the sergeant walk back to his car and deposit the box in the boot before climbing into the front seat and drive off, giving a wave as he passed by.

"Ru, do you mind if we put the chair in the boot so I don't have it sticking into my back on the way home like I did when we came here," Steve asked.

"No problemo Stevey-boy. You know I've never had to put the back seat down on the Audi before ever since I've bought it."

"Here, help me up," Steve said as he held his hand out.

Ru pulled him up almost as easily as if he was a weight at the gym and once up he leant onto the car to steady himself.

"Take this top cover down here by unhooking it….then press that button on the left. You see, you don't have to put the whole seat back, I only need that section," Steve explained.

Ru leant forward and pushed a section of the seat down and started folding up the wheelchair when something caught Steve's attention. In the crack that appeared between the base of the folded seat and the cover of the boot Steve could see something red and white that seemed out of place.

"Before you put the chair away, can you help me with something?" he asked.

"Sure thing… what's up?" Ru said, as a flake of snow landed on her nose.

"Pull up the floor of the boot".

"Really, you can do that?" Ru asked.

Steve nodded.

"It's where you spare tyre and toolset are if you get a puncture." he explained.

"Oh ok, I always just fluttered my eyelids and swooned at hot guys when that happened in the old one" she chortled.

"Yeah, I remember", Steve laughed.

As Ru pulled back the grey hardboard floor cover, her mouth dropped white open.

"Oh my God!"

"Holy Fu….." Steve tailed off.

Before their eyes was an entire car boot full of £50 notes. They covered the whole floor and the wheel well where the tyre should have been. Ru put her hand in, the money was deeper than the length of her fingers and in fasted in wads by rubber bands. She picked one out and started counting.

"50,100, 150, 200, 250, 300, 350, 400, 450, 500" she cried.

"It's Mikey's money. He must have known that not only would you never check your car but that you'd never, ever let anyone else touch it either. Nor would it fall under suspicion from any one who might be after him". Steve mused

Ru held the wad of notes and smelt it, rubbed the sides on her cheek before running her fingers over the aluminium anti-forgery strip. She'd never seen more than a handful of fifties in her life.

"If his plan had worked, he would have taken the money back and you'd never have been the wiser", continued Steve.

"I wonder how much is here?" Ru asked.

"Millions. You're rich Ru!"

"You mean WE are rich Stevey-boy."

"We can buy any house we want. We can start up our own investigative company like we talked about."

"Steve and Ru's Private Detective Agency". Steve screamed with delight.

"You mean Ru and Steve's Vigilante Corporation!", she countered.

"Wow, this is going to change our lives. We can help so many people with this," she said as she tossed the money nonchalantly back into the boot before throwing the cover back.

"If you have a problem, if no-one else can help you. Maybe you can call the aRSe team" Steve laughed.

Ru lifted the wheelchair into the boot and closed the door before helping Steve into the front passenger seat. Jumping into the drivers seat, she turned the key in the ignition, revved up the engine and pumped up the volume on the radio.

"Let's go and kick some ass!' She shouted as the car roared off sending gravel spewing into the air behind them.

*   *   *

At the rear of the church car park, a solitary figure took off his dark sunglasses and wiped them clean with his handkerchief. What a lucky break it was seeing the listing of the funeral in the newspaper. This was the start he needed.

He went back into his phone and checked that the photos had come out clearly and breathed a sigh of relief he saw they he had everything he needed, at least for now.

Placing his glasses back over his eyes, he started his car engine. He knew he had to report his findings and hopefully in a few weeks he would be duly rewarded.

The End

Vixen will return in V2 - Vengeance

About The Author

Stephen Liddell lives in Hertfordshire, England and has been a great fan of the pulp noir and vigilante genre since the early 1980's which was no doubt far too young for the film certifications of the time.

Inspired by movies such as the Death Wish series and strong female characters such as Lara Croft and Buffy The Vampire Slayer, Stephen mixed everything together to create V with the London area providing a rich and endless canvas.

Stephen has written a number of conventional history books including, Lest We Forget: A Concise Companion to the First World War, which was published in 2014 by Endeavour Press of London and is available in Kindle and Paperback formats and a wry, humorous look at tortures with 101 Most Horrible Tortures In History.

If you enjoyed V1, before V2 comes out then you might like to read The Promise, book one of the Timeless Trilogy.

Stephen has also written a number of historical novels and a humorous travelogue of true-life backpacking adventures. As a long time affection-ado of the horror genre, he watched his first 18 rated Horror movie 'Halloween' at the age of six and has penned a script entitled 'Playground of Terror' which is due to be filmed as part of the GoryTime TV series later in 2016.

He regularly updates his blog at www.stephenliddell.co.uk and contributes to magazines on historical, social and environmental issues as well as occasional media appearances.

You can email Stephen at stephenliddell@gmail.com or follow him on Twitter at https://twitter.com/Stephen_Liddell or like his Facebook page. Don't forget to Like the V Trilogy Page to keep up to date with all the news and events for Vixen as book 2 approaches.

Stephen also runs and personally guides Ye Olde England Tours which provides private and bespoke tours to the Western Front as well as in London and around southern England. www.yeoldeenglandtours.co.uk   If you like V please do leave a nice review as every author values each and every one of them. :-)

Lightning Source UK Ltd.
Milton Keynes UK
UKHW011839100521
383500UK00001B/26